THE OLD TERRA VITAE

By Paddy Green

Cover image derived from "Burrard and Smithe Trolleybus Wires" by Roland Tanglao under a Creative Commons License., with thanks.

Thanks for the support!

Paddy

W0006675

COPYRIGHT

The Old Terra Vitae

Copyright: Patrick Green

Published: 1st December 2012

ISBN: 978-1-291-22370-5

DEDICATION

For Heather and for Henson My favourite pair of
H-Bombs

Truth be told, your soul was sold,
The moment you placed your bet
Ten minutes late, you tempted fate,
And we're calling in the debt,
So stand there at the edge of the platform,
Close your eyes and let nature take it's course,
Gravity, your old enemy,
That old universal law will pull you down,

You should never bet on one,
'Cause my dice has been loaded to roll a six,
I'm afraid this fight was fixed,
But then again, aren't they all,
If you paint the devil on the wall,
The devil's gonna come.

Look at what I'm showing you,
Optical illusions and visual lies,
Visualise your space and time,
You don't have much of either,
Look at what I'm offering,
An opportunity like none before,
One step forward and one step more,
And let physics do the rest.

- Zvilnik, "Paint The Devil On The Wall"
(http://zvilnik.co.uk)

PROLOGUE

The End Is Just The Beginning

I really thought it was over, but apparently I wasn't that lucky. The whole thing was like something from an eighties straight-to-VHS movie. After the feedback whine of my demise faded, after the black fingers of the grave closed in on my mind and I felt the warm buzz of consciousness spin off into the distance leaving me enveloped in a comfortable cloak of non-existence, I only went and woke up.

I must have been out for a while, because the morning sun had been replaced with the purple haze of twilight, and it had got a lot colder. My head was resting on a damp clump of weedy grass, and I felt vaguely damp all over. My muscles were stiff to my core, and it took a real effort of will to creak into a sitting position and take a proper look around the now deserted field. My eyes didn't want to focus, and I had to shake my head to rattle them loose, clearing my clouded vision.

So there I was, sat down in a muddy field, cold ground mist creeping up around my legs and arse. Everyone else was gone, the van was gone, Eliza was gone. The gallows were gone. It was just me, sat in the clumpy grass, bemused and freezing cold and trying to work out where everyone else had disappeared to. Not that I was sad they'd gone, they weren't the friendliest mob of vengeance-obsessed maniacs I'd ever encountered. I could see the city rising up out of the twilight skyline, it's usual form interrupted by a giant square monolith of a building. Something was very strange here. I picked myself up and started walking. It took longer than I thought it would to reach civilisation.

Cold fields turned to a deserted suburbia, and finally to the inner city. I kept myself pointed at the large building that sprouted from the city's heart, which called to me like some kind of beacon, but the streets were like some kind of screwed up labyrinth, confounding my sense of direction and constantly steering me away from my destination. I pushed on, sensing figures waiting just out of sight in the mist, eyeing me as I stumbled around the place. Offering myself up as a sacrifice, a lost lamb in the domain of the hungry wolves. Fresh meat for the feast.

I tried to keep the rising panic down, and kept aligning myself on my goal, trying to not look too appetising, but I could sense that the figures in the mist had got my number. I attempted to find shelter, some place to regroup, but the doors to all of the buildings were either locked or just painted on, a facade on some kind of oversized film set. Each door that I tried was a knock to my credibility, a registered loan application being rejected and making my credit rating even worse - and something told me the loan sharks in this place would be repossessing more than just my flat screen TV and laptop.

The wolves were closing in, and I started to move faster, despite my exhaustion. I tried not to break into a run - there are rules I've known my whole life and that's one of them. Shadows darted across the gaping mouths of alleyways, monsters keeping pace on the parallel streets, waiting for me to lose it, waiting for me to offer myself up as dinner. Then I saw the figure on all fours beneath the streetlight up ahead, its muzzle drooling and pooling saliva on the pavement. The sodium light illuminated its canines, gleaming hungrily in the mist.

My instincts told me there was no turning back in this place, so I kept going, each step bringing me closer to the monstrous apparition, and then I was stood close enough to touch it. I could smell the foul stench of its mangy fur, almost taste its sulphurous breath as it misted from its flared nostrils.

"Alright there fella", it barked, "Name's Juju. I'm gonna be looking after you for a bit. Show you the ropes, help you get acclimatised, shall we say? Let's get a drink, shall we?"

CHAPTER ONE

On The Fear Of Things That Don't Exist

For his whole life, Loupe was scared of things that don't exist. He clearly remembered that when he'd been to the toilet as a little kid, he absolutely had to get to the bottom of the stairs before the flush noise had finished, or the monster in the airing cupboard would burst from his prison and drag him away to some netherworld beyond the towels. He nearly broke his neck on several occasions taking that staircase three at a time, consumed with terror. He'd look up and feel a frisson of fear when he walked under a loft hatch, some part of him expecting to find it opened a mysterious crack by a lurking horror.

In the house, there was a skylight on the landing, which allowed light in from another one in the roof. The glass was coloured and clouded, and afforded a broken and difficult view into the attic. He found himself glancing at it, furtively, as he went upstairs. He didn't know what he expected - monsters again, he supposed, looking back down at him. The blank stare of some

Korean horror movie ghost child, perhaps. He watched too many of those movies.

And that was the thing: that fear had been a part of his life for so long that he began to embrace it, even need it sometimes. So he watched his horror movies in the dark. He turned off the lights, and sat in a chair in the middle of the room, so his back was exposed. He opened the doors, so the creeping things that constantly watched for their chance to take him away had every opportunity to do their worst. He courted their claws and even though they never took him up on his invitation, even though they never proved their existence after years of chances... he was still afraid of them. He'd stand up from his bed in the middle of the night, and try to be cool and grown up about it, but the first few steps were still a scuttle to escape their cold fingers before he got a grip on himself, and felt embarrassed.

The fear only came when he was alone, so was probably rooted in some childhood fear of abandonment. Separation anxiety, they call it these days. The whole thing could probably be explained by two minutes with a copy of Pop Psychology For Dummies, even - and he knew that, he knew it was all just a trick his brain played on itself, just something his brain made up because he was left with a soiled nappy for a little too long one night, but his lizard brain... well that brain knew different. The lizard brain knew that what he was scared of was monsters - very real, very wicked, and driven by motivations alien to our own.

Of course, now Loupe knows better, now he's seen what happens backstage, and despite knowing the tricks, and knowing how monstrous shadows can be cast on reality with nothing more than the post-mortem equivalent of a candle and a cardboard puppet - he still gets that fear. If anything, it comes even worse now, when it does come, because he knows for certain that the world he saw then was just one part of what was really out there, that the limits of the universe went far beyond what he could see and touch. If that was the case with that old, discarded life, if the old terra vitae was just a paper-thin construct just waiting for something to reach through... he figured all bets were off from here on in.

Anyway, there's only so much introspection one man can take before he gets his mind all folded up, and these days Loupe has plenty more to worry about than why he's scared of the dark. As of today he got a third black mark from the authority (I believe they prefer that with a capital A, and omitting that big respectful letter is one of those little acts of rebellion that make me feel a bit better about myself). It doesn't even matter why he got it, since as far as he can tell the rules are arbitrary and made up at any given moment to suit their needs. It's to be expected, since the whole thing is a matter of entropy.

You know how, when you move to a new town, the whole place starts as kind of a maze? There are streets that seem straight as you head down them but somehow bring you out far closer to where you started than you expected. You're never going in the direction you think you are, and wherever you end up is never where you planned on being. Over time, though, you expand your movements out from your new home base, and the map solidifies - you pull order out of the chaos and you forget that you could ever get lost in this new place.

You see, out here things are a bit looser, a lot more changeable - the geography of the whole place is kind of fluid. Hell, even the physics aren't set in stone. A lot of folks find it hard to handle, and bounce around the place like malfunctioning helicopters, just freaking out. People who never saw round the corners back home. It's the ones who were so utterly confident in whatever their worldview happened to be that fall apart, the devout believer, the equally devout atheist.

The ones who knew their rules, and saw how their reality and those rules fit together with righteous clarity - and that's more people than you think. Most of us simply don't have the time or the inclination to doubt the way things really operate, no matter how much we like to insist we do. Anyway, the rising tide of chaos takes them pretty quickly; I just sometimes wish they'd be a little quieter about it.

The fear, though - I reckon that's what has helped Loupe keep it together back here. That part of me spent so long insisting that nothing was what it seemed, so once he ended up here it was like a vindication. His rational mind knew better, maybe, but that paranoid, frightened lower brain took over for a while and taught him to cope with the new environment - it showed him how to fit in, and how to navigate this alien space. After a few years (which he claims he doesn't remember, conveniently enough for him) his more coherent faculties could resurface, and you could say he was reborn. Of course that's just my opinion - but as Loupe's therapist, I'd say I'm pretty qualified.

They call me the Juju Puppy, and Loupe considers me opinionated - not to mention scabrous, rude, and altogether unpleasant - but you take what you can in the way of friends back here. I'm a licensed therapist and grief counsellor, and I have this terrible habit of invoicing him for the time we spend together. Loupe suspects this is just my own private joke, because he's never paid the bills and we still hang out. I'm a terrible alcoholic, and have a tendency to spit bits of half digested kibble around the place when I talk - too much, in Loupe's opinion. Oh yeah, and I drool a bit, though only on the left side. What do you expect? I'm a dog after all.

Anyway, my actual professional opinion of Loupe is that he's basically just a massive pussy (to use the technical therapist word for people like him). By which I mean that he is the embodiment (or maybe disembodiment) of that old cliché, the lost soul who can't move on - the trapped spirit with the unfinished business. I'm right, of course, but that doesn't mean Loupe takes that kind of abuse from me, all smug about it as I dribble into my whiskey. So why does this make him a massive pussy?

Well, the problem isn't the unfinished business - the problem is that he's spent the last god knows how long here not dealing with the business. Instead he's been working for the authority, and building up credit to drink here with me, and doing everything he can to avoid the business. And the reason he's avoiding the business is to do with everything I've been saying up to now... he's afraid. He's deathly, sickeningly, shit-his-pants afraid to the point that all he can do is pretend the business doesn't exist and hope it will go away - which is akin to trying to wish the moon would go away. You can spend all night wishing as hard as you like, and then the morning comes and it's like your wish came true, but then the earth turns again and you're back where you started, because some things are just too big to ignore forever.

Of course, it hasn't gone away, and unfortunately for Loupe, that means it time for a patented Juju Puppy intervention, and things are about to get a whole lot worse. Which is saying a lot when you factor in that so far:

Loupe's infant son was horribly murdered by an invisible monster from beyond the grave, an event which lead to Loupe learning that the police and press and even your own wife don't tend to believe explanations involving invisible monsters, and found himself at the centre of a whirlwind of hate mail and media witch-huntery, culminating in his being (very painfully) torn to pieces by a crazed mob of social media grief athletes who'd clubbed together to make him pay for the crime they thought he'd committed - a demise which sent him spiralling into an afterlife where the poor bugger still needs a job to afford the bar tab from drinking too much whiskey with a mangy ghost dog with an attitude problem.

The problem is, you see, that invisible monster. Because I know who he is, and I have a fair suspicion that Loupe's unfinished business isn't half as unfinished as he thinks it is - what happened to his son, what happened to him - that was only the beginning, and if you have any idea how things work round here, that means that he's one of very few people with any chance of doing anything about it. And there's another part of his scared lizard brain, a part that doesn't need to remember what happened to scream bloody vengeance for the part of him that was left broken on a nursery floor, because the code for that is written all the way through the meat and bones in genetic binary. Rest in peace? Fat chance.

This place is like a bad drawing, really, and it's been drawn on cheap-ass paper with low quality Chinese wax crayons to boot - someone in a hurry has been tracing over the real world, creating a dodgy copy of it. Everywhere there is represented here, just badly. It's the basis of the job, finding ways in any given location to reach across that gap from the rough simulation back here into the base reality of it, to tweak things, throw things, and upset the apple cart. It's mostly just an act of will, really. You impose yourself on reality and break some shit.

But that's Loupe's job - he makes changes. Every day he gets a docket, a sneaky to-do list of things to move, of elbows to nudge. He navigates his way to the right place and the right time, and does the business. The net effect on human history of the changes he makes is precisely nil, and to be honest I find it hard to even see why his job exists - but there's no shortage of people doing pointless activities day in and day out in order to pull down a pay packet, and frankly this place doesn't offer an overwhelming variety of career options. Loupe doesn't have the entrepreneurial spirit to go freelance like me, so I spends his days doing the bidding of the Authority. He punches his card, and he pays his dues.

This week, for example, he's nudged twenty-three different sets of keys out of pockets and into assorted nooks and crannies, causing folks to be a couple of minutes later than normal for their usual routines. Thanks to those missed minutes, people haven't bumped into an old friend in their morning commute, who would have held them up in conversation, changing their daily schedule by a further twenty or more minutes. The events that could have happened in those twenty minutes all happen differently. The ebb and flow of humanity around that person on that day completely changes - diseases follow different vectors, people meet future spouses they would never have met, leading to births that would never have happened. The whole world is a different place, because of a set of keys being moved.

You'd think this would be pretty exciting stuff - changing the entire face of the planet sounds like an amazing job, right? But like I say - it isn't really different, it all manages to bend itself back into shape in the end - the changes are sweeping but ultimately inconsequential. They say the changes are keeping things as they should be - correcting variations from a bigger plan, but I can't see it myself. My personal theory is that these people are deluded, but if they want to pay Loupe to help them, who in turn pays for my drinks, then as far as I'm concerned they can believe anything they want. They're throwing paint at a wall and hoping it will randomly form the Mona Lisa. The Authority and their employees are, in effect, monkeys trying to randomly generate Shakespeare by throwing rocks at a sea of typewriters.

I try not to think about it - the weight of futility is enough to drive a man to drink. Which reminds me, I'm late for my appointment with Loupe, and he hates it when I'm late. I'll tell him I couldn't find my keys.

CHAPTER TWO

A Prelude To A Night Of Excessive Drinking

"Hi Loupe, I'm quite sure it's your round. It's pretty much the least you can do, on account of your continuing non-payment of your ever-expanding therapy bill". I like to change up my accent over time, introduce new elements, let it evolve - at the moment it's kind of a cross between South African, Glaswegian and Egyptian - it keeps people on their toes.

"Hey Juju", he sighs, resigned to another night of funding my drinking problem. "Usual, right?". Naturally, he's already one step ahead, and I hop onto the stool and hit the straw. He looks down. I don't mean he looks down like dogs can't look up, I mean he looks depressed. That's another technical therapist word for you right there. Also, when he's talking to me, he kind of has to look down, because I'm smaller than he is. He picks up his drink, and we get down to business.

He's a funny looking customer, is Loupe - pale, drawn, big hair. If he was a woman, and alive, then Tim Burton would probably marry him and spend the rest of his life putting him in movies. He always looks like he's on the brink of crying, throwing up, or crying and throwing up. He looks like he hasn't slept in five years, making a mockery of the popular phrase "you can sleep when you're dead". His clothes just kind of hang on him like they've been sentenced to being worn. He's crumpled and creased, and thoroughly deceased.

"So, favourite client 'o mine", I smutter at him (always try to keep it upbeat, that's my motto), "how's your day been? Ready for a night you'll regret tomorrow? Or even better, ready for a night you'll forget tomorrow?"

Loupe doesn't reply, draining his glass. A gesture to the barman, and another pair of drinkies arrives. So it's going to be one of those nights, then. I quickly suck up the last of drink number one, and we get down to serious business. He won't have anything to say for a while. We'll just drink, and I'll talk - if you haven't gathered I'm pretty good at filling in the silences - but that's just part of my system.

Eventually, we'll reach his tipping point - everything will click into place, and then the real work begins. It's a good job I'm an excellent drinker. This barman does have an annoying tendency to take the empties away, though - I like to see them stack up, like they would in a movie to indicate the inebriation of the protagonists. Well, you can imagine that if you like. Imagine a lot of those empty tumblers, stacked two high. Loupe doesn't look at me, he looks at a thousand reflections of himself in your imaginary glass-pile when he finally speaks;

"I can't do this anymore, man. I know you keep saying I'm stuck here, that I won't face it. But what am I supposed to do? I'm stuck in an arse-end of an afterlife, doing a job I wouldn't have put up with when I was alive. You're right. I've got to move on."

"Amen, broth-", he doesn't give me a chance to even encourage him. Boy's on a roll.

"So where do I start? How do I get out of here, Juju?"

"It's like I al-"

"I guess it's like you always say, I have to understand the past to face the future." He's right, I do always say that.

"I do, but you have to rem-"

"I just have to remember. What happened, I mean."

"Well, we could us-"

"Why don't we use some of that regression therapy you're always banging on about. Or, I dunno, maybe we could use one of those psychic guys from the district, but I dunno, could you take a psychic seriously...?", he trailed off.

"People take Stephen Hawking seriously."

"He's a physicist."

"Right. Yeah. So, why don't we just go there and then? We'll go and look, see what happened."

"No fucking way, Juju. No way on earth.", he's vehement - I don't think I can push him on this one. He falls silent again.

"So hypnotism, that's really a real thing, is it?"

"Real as you and me."

"Well, that's open for debate, since you're a talking dog who claims to be a licensed therapist."

"You'll just have to take my word for it. You're real, I'm real, hypnotism is really real. We'll just go and look at some other stuff first, we'll build you up to it, OK?"

He signals the barman, and more drinks arrive. Down in one, a beat and... exhale.

"So what do we do?"

"Right now, we keep drinking. We wait a few days - you make sure you're ready."

"I'm ready now."

There's a pause. Believe it or not, I'm proud of him. It may seem like the bravado of the booze-sodden, the conversation where you declare you're going to be best mates for the rest of your days and fuck it, let's pack in our jobs tomorrow and buy a bus and take off to Bolivia or somewhere 'cause you know what you're my best mate and Bolivia isn't just going to come to us. And maybe that's a part of it, but he's never got this far on any of our marathon drinking sessions before, so maybe I won't need that patented Juju Puppy intervention after all.

Oh wait, no, I already did it.

In fact, the intervention has been going on for the last week. Carefully placed signs setting subliminal ideas in Loupe's mind. Overheard conversations between people who maybe weren't there by accident. Memos distributed around his office, with coded messages that he wouldn't notice consciously, but that his subconscious happily translated and added to the pile of psychological emails I spent the last week sending directly to Loupe's brain, all with one basic message - "get your thumb out of your arse and get on with getting on." Well, I told you I was good. Now it's time to help this wreck of a wraith find his way to the inevitable conclusion - but that's a job for tomorrow.

"I'm sure you are, Loupe, but still. Tonight we'll have a few more drinks, and leave some dribble on the bar. Who knows, we might even make a clean spot."

"And then...?"

"Then we wait, like I say, for a few days. Let you get your shit together. Get prepared."

"And then...?"

"And then we get into it. We go back to figure out what happened, see if you can put a face to that 'invisible monster' of yours."

"And then."

"And then, assuming we manage to dig through the puzzle box that is your brain, we talk about what you DO about it. We talk about practical steps. Self-actualisation. Other psychological therapist sounding words and phrases."

"You're a consummate professional."

"Which is why you always pay your bills on time. In opposite world. Seriously, if you're not ready for this, if you're not psychologically prepared, you're going to take a fall at the last hurdle."

I tell Loupe a story, to illustrate my point.

"There was a young man, of modest means but not poverty-stricken, who awoke as he did every morning, and visited the bathroom to drain himself. It was a long piss. Now ask yourself this - how long would you need to urinate before you started to worry? You'd be surprised how quickly you'd get concerned. Of course, you've never measured how long it takes you to have a piss, but it doesn't take long before you're saying "Ha ha, it's Miller time".

"My point is, even after a minute, you'd be worried - and that's what happened to the young man in our tale. A minute of micturition and our hero was already getting nervous. Five minutes and the flow was still showing no signs of abatement. Fifteen minutes, and panic was starting to set in.

"He called the NHS helpline on his mobile. They'd never heard of such a thing - it was impossible, surely? You can't just keep pissing for half an hour (because yes, it was half an hour by this point), there simply isn't enough room for that much fluid in the human body, so there's no way this can be happening. Thank you, stop wasting our time, get off the line. Another half hour passes. He's in tears, with no idea what's happening to him. He's sat down now, urinating like a lady and trying to formulate a plan. Finally, he dials the emergency services, and is told an ambulance will be dispatched immediately. He waits, but no ambulance comes. Clearly they didn't take his call seriously and dropped him into the crank-list.

"Finally, he takes matters into his own hands. Not even caring about his carpets anymore, he stands and leaves the bathroom. Piss runs down his trouser legs, and trickles over his shoes. He squelches down the stairs, out of the front door, and into the street. There is no way he'll be able to get a cab or a bus while in this state of full flow, so he sets off walking towards the hospital. Another hour, during which litres and litres of impossible piss flood from his apparently demented body.

Into the emergency room, where he is immediately ushered outside again. The nurses watch in puzzlement as he continues to leak. Towels are brought to absorb the excess, before he's popped in a wheelchair and rolled in to see the doctor. The doctor listens to his story as he sits in an ever expanding pile of urine soaked towels, before opening a drawer and pulling out a small plastic container. Which he hands to the boy.

"Immediately the flow stops. He takes the pot, and looks at the doctor, at the nurses gathered around him. He stands and walks into the adjoining bathroom, opens his soaked trousers and aims at the plastic vessel. Not even a drop. He can sense them all on the other side of the door and can't even manage one tiny millilitre.

"He emerges, red faced. "I think you're going to have to squeeze it out of a towel", he mutters."

Loupe looks at me like I've crapped in his cornflakes. Yeah, the story doesn't quite gel, hell, it doesn't even make sense - doesn't matter, I've got his mind to back off for a moment. More drinks? Don't mind if I do.

"OK. A couple of days, then... you can help me?"

"Yeah, Loupe. I can help you. I'm your therapist, aren't I? Not only that, but I'm the best there is - the creme de la crematorium, you might say. Helping you is my job. Now line 'em up - we're going to make sure you have the worst possible day at work tomorrow."

And that's exactly what we do. We drink like monsters, like men possessed. The kind of drinking that should lead to a trip to A&E. Once the barman cut us off, and strictly speaking he should have cut us off long before he did, we call him some very rude names and stumble off into the night, our separate ways. I pause at the corner, and turn to watch Loupe bouncing off street furniture as he disappears into the constant vague fog of this place. Poor bastard.

I turn and head for home, seeing the monolithic Authority building towering out of the grey mist in front of me. I hate that building - it's stacked too high and hangs around like it owns the place. It's a big mean old self-important bully of a building, outstaying its welcome on the skyline of the afterlife, and the people who run it aren't much better in my experience.

They're the kind of people who use the words task and action as verbs, and then verbify the word verb so they can use the word verbify. Being dead should be fun, surely? Not with these guys about, making up phrases like "chunking the elephant" when they want to break up a big job, hiding their layers of bureaucracy under obfuscating blankets of fictional language.

They hate freelancers like me, the people who live outside their system, outside their weird obsessive compulsive plans and schemes. I put my head down, trying to avoid eye contact with it, in case looking at it might draw me into their way of life. I felt bad enough that I'd got Loupe a job there in the first place - though what can you do with a freshly minted corpse with a limited skill set? At least he got access to the staff canteen, which by all accounts does an excellent moussaka.

I turn the next corner and find myself face to face with someone I really didn't want to see. It's Pilter, his pockmarked face buried in the disgusting crochet scarf everyone assumes he found in a bin. Clearly he's as surprised to see me as I am him, but he pulls the scarf down over his chin, letting it scrape on his hobo stubble, and grins a foul and snaggletoothed grin. He knows full well that I really don't want to see him - and he knows full well why, and his eyes light up in malicious glee because he knows he's got me on the hook.

"Well, look who it is. Long time no see, JuJu!"

"Pilter."

"So what's been happening? Anything new to report?"

"Same old, same old." I shrug my haunches, doggy style.

"Yeah, same here, same. Cold night."

"Aren't they all? Look, I gotta go, it's late and-"

"Absolutely, brother, say no more. You have a good night."

I edge past him, painfully aware of the gleam in his eye. Pilter has always been trouble, a snitch of the worst order, and in with people I didn't really want to be in contact with at the moment. Continuing down the street, I cast an eye back and see him standing there, watching me go. He shouts down the road after me. Son of a bitch was just waiting 'til I thought I was in the clear before reeling me in.

"Hey, one thing before you go!" - I stop.

"What is it, Pilter?"

"Last I heard, The Mouse was looking for you - apparently you didn't leave a forwarding address, and I think he said something about... delivering some mail or something?", he snickered audibly.

"I'll make sure I give him a call then."

"Well, how about you tell me where he can find you - I think he's pretty keen to have a little catch up. You know how he hates it when he loses touch with his friends. I'm happy to pass on the address for you, we're pretty tight, me and The Mouse."

"Thanks for the offer, Pilter, but you know me, I'd rather apologise in person for being so lax about updating my contact information. The personal touch makes all the difference."

"It sure does. Why don't we go and see him now? We'll share a cab."

"Look, just tell him I have a good client who's going to pay me soon, and then he'll be the first person on my list regarding back rent."

I turn, and walk off down the street, furtively glancing over my shoulder as I go. Unsurprisingly, Pilter follows me at a menacing amble. I stop, and he leans against the wall, whistling. When I reach the next corner, I put my head down and sprint a couple of side alleys before taking refuge behind some bins. Pilter comes careening pell-mell down the alley after me, straight past my hiding place. He's sneaky and sly, that one, but he's never been particularly sharp. I'm going to have to be very careful, though, the last thing I need right now is an encounter with The Mouse - he's a much brighter spark, and so sharp you could very easily get cut - and that was a very narrow squeak.

CHAPTER THREE

Nothing Good Ever Happens At Four In The Morning

Of all the things that annoyed Loupe about his job, it was punching in that really chapped his crack - it just seemed so redundant, and downright unfair. If anything should earn a man a little downtime, it was being dead, surely? Nonetheless, the next day he dragged his ragged and very sorry self into the office, and punched his card like he always did.

Other agents passed in and out, but Loupe had never bothered to learn their faces or names - usually they weren't around for that long. Loupe, on the other hand, was starting to feel like he'd be here forever, without even the comforting glimmer of hope that one day he'd be dead and not have to get his rumpled, stained carcass into this place every morning.

His desk, one of those metal jobs that have been the mainstay of cop shows since the 1970's, was pretty much bare. No photos, no plastic dancing hula girl. Just a couple of folders with the day's dockets sitting in them - little things to be moved a little way for little purpose. He sat, then collapsed forward and pressed his forehead hard against the cold steel surface, until he could feel the texture of the table imprinting itself on him. He took a deep breath, forced the daily bile back down his throat.

He rose again from the desk, felt his now bumpy forehead, and scanned around. It wasn't just the desk that had the seventies vibe - the whole place looked like something from a TV show. No computers, nothing modern at all - grey metal filing cabinets and brown plywood dividers with wobbly glass panels. A linoleum floor in a fetching shade of dusty green, stained and scuffed and full of trip hazards. He picked up the first folder, and checked the docket. Same old thing, coordinates and a description of the item to be shifted - this time a mobile phone. No more instructions because the instructions were always the same - get it somewhere where it's not supposed to be - down the side of a cushion, under the sofa, whatever.

"Whatever", muttered Loupe. He picked up the docket, stuffed it in his pocket, and headed for the door.

A convoluted stream of trains and cars and plain old footwork followed, his head down and his belly protesting the whole way, but eventually Loupe found himself outside a nondescript house in a nondescript sodium-lit street. He didn't bother to knock, and walked straight through the door, checking his watch as he did. The darkened house loomed around him. Somebody had once said to him that nothing good happens at four in the morning, and they were right. Then again, nothing good ever happened to Loupe, it seemed. He headed up the stairs.

A lone figure lay in the bed, snoring softly. Loupe engaged burglar mode and tiptoed into the room, not that it made any difference. Even if the man had been awake, he wouldn't have seen Loupe as he crept across the insufficiently vacuumed carpet, and around to the far side of the bed. The guy was a slob - the discarded clothes of several days lay scattered about the place, and Loupe could see a collection of mugs building up under the side of the bed. Good news for Loupe, since it would make it all the easier for the phone to get lost.

The phone sat on a bedside table, one lone LED blinking like some baleful, watching eye - drinking up charge from a cable snaking from beneath. Loupe reached forward and concentrated, pressing one clammy palm against the phone screen before batting at the cable with his other hand. That was how it was done - you could only perform broad strokes, and they weren't terribly effective - like a cat with a ball on a piece of string, precision was never on the agenda. The cable popped out of its housing and curled away down the side of the bed. A good start. Now to deal with the phone itself.

The tendency in recent years was for larger phones, which was a problem - larger also meant heavier, and while a few grams meant very little in reality, this meant a whole lot more physical effort in a haunt. Loupe scanned the surroundings, looking for the ideal cranny to push the phone into - and decided that if he went for the gap between the table and the bed, there was a good chance the phone would go under and bounce behind the growing mug collection, giving him the few minutes change in his target's schedule he was aiming for. It was going to require a big push, though.

He steeled himself, and took a deep breath - in and out like a sniper waiting for the ideal moment to strike, like Tiger Woods addressing the ball. He swung back, tried to focus all of his physicality into the tip of his left hand, and then scooped down and struck the phone like a hockey puck.

Normally this would be enough to move the phone a couple of inches, tipping it over the edge and allowing it to fall and bounce into it's new position under the bed - but not this time. The phone took off like Loupe had fired it out of a catapult, hitting the headboard of the bed with an audible crack as the screen hit the wooden frame, then rebounded onto the head of the unfortunate sleeper below, who awoke with a start - that is to say as if a starting pistol had been fired next to his head.

The target sat bolt upright in bed, and Loupe froze as he fumbled around for the light switch and flooded the room with lamplight. His statue impression was entirely unnecessary, since the target could no more see him than he could see his own farts. Still, it's a natural instinct that very few people manage to get over, even when they've been doing this job for years. The man looked around, bleary, and Loupe almost thought the man's eyes settled on him before casting him off as a shadow, and finding instead his broken phone sitting on the duvet in front of him, half of the screen hanging out of the casing and looking altogether very sorry for itself. The man cursed as he stumbled into consciousness and tried to make sense of what was in front of him.

Quickly, Loupe turned and made a dash from the room, and sprinted, panicked, down the stairs two at a time, before running through the front door. Or at least he should have gone through the front door, which decided to offer more resistance than it should have. The crashing reverberated round the house's four in the morning silence, which is well known for being able to amplify even the quietest of sounds.

Loupe picked himself up, his face a mask of Norman Wisdomesque comic surprise. A man walks into a bar, he thought out of nowhere. Tentatively he reached forward and pushed at the door, this time finding the comforting familiarity of being able to pass through its solid, unyielding construction - and in moments he was out, and running for the train station. Sighing, he pulled the dockets from his pockets, screwed them up and tossed them.

INTERLUDE ONE

The Goldfish Keeping Habits Of Mark Benson

An ordinary man, with an ordinary life. Mark Benson never did anything to harm anyone. He lived alone, with only a tank containing three large goldfish for company. The fish, lacking the ability to wipe, each trailed a tail of fishy excrement behind them as they swam in their roomy tank. Occasionally one of them would bump the tail of another, and the fishy poo would float in the tank before sinking to the bottom to sit around on the gravel until Mark changed the water and cleaned the whole thing up.

Mark always noticed when one of his fish had lost their revolting trail, and although all three fish looked exactly alike, he could always tell them apart. He never gave them names though - they were fish, and he ascribed no personality to them and felt no real affection. He simply found their simple lives relaxing to observe, as they drifted about in the glass prison that they dutifully accepted.

It was Mark's birthday, and he was due to meet some of his friends. They were going bowling, and he found bowling tolerable. He found his friends likeable enough, though secretly he thought of them more as colleagues than friends. Most of the time, he thought of people a bit like he thought of his three goldfish - with no real strong feeling, but it was relaxing to know they were there, to observe their rituals and join in at the appropriate points.

He certainly didn't feel like he was missing out, or that his life was a lesser thing for this. He took part, he performed the social equivalent of cleaning out the tank. People thought he was caring because he noticed when they got new haircuts, or when the events in their lives wrought changes in their personalities - but that was just like how he always noticed when one of his fishes lost their poo tail.

You might think of Mark as being a little odd, with his socially awkward ways and his seemingly stunted ability to relate to others, but you shouldn't judge him too harshly. He was always well aware of his social shortcomings, and tried hard to be a part of things, to show willing to participate. It's true that he was rarely drawn into any in-depth conversations, and that he often agreed with others maybe a little too willingly, not wanting to rock the boat, not wishing to offend - but maybe that wasn't such a bad thing. He liked his fish, and he liked watching their lives revolve around their tank, and for Mark Benson, that was more than enough.

As Mark walked to his car to head to the bowling alley, he didn't notice the subtle force that tugged at his shoelace, almost imperceptibly. If he had, he would probably have tied the lace up again. Instead he got into his car, and set off for his night out with the people he called friends.

Mark's life would have changed that night, because one of his friends (Rob, a man from the IT department with a slightly lazy eye who did great impressions of famous comedians at office parties) brought a girl with him. Her name was Pamela, and for Mark meeting her would have been like a flatlander suddenly seeing the world in eye-popping three dee.

In their conversations that evening, he would have discovered that she also kept goldfish, and was secretly fascinated by their trails of hanging poop. That night would have been like he was an inflatable man, previously empty and hanging from a hook, suddenly inflated - brought to life in three dimensions, a truly life changing event. Mark would have started to see the whole world differently, the interior lives of his friends brought magically into the open, their opinions and ideas no longer a mystery to him as if a blindfold was taken from his eyes. Pamela would prove to be the key that unlocked his dormant humanity.

Further meetings would have followed that night, and before long their goldfish would have been living in a shared tank, and Mark and Pamela would have a running joke about who was the first to spot a broken tail. When one of the fish died, they would know which one it was, and Pamela would make a little gravestone for it with it's name on, and they would bury it in the garden.

Mark and Pamela were undeniably perfect for each other, and their story would have been a happy one. Their goldfish were soon joined by twins, who they called Henry and Arabella, and they spent many happy years together, each complementing the other's strengths and almost never arguing - and when they did argue, it was never something they couldn't resolve.

Their house was a happy home, a picture of christmas card perfection. After many years of wedded bliss, after their children had grown and gone (but visited often, bringing their beautiful grandchildren, who adored them and loved to watch the fish) they relaxed into a peaceful old age, before gently drifting off together one night to a sleep from which neither would wake. Mark and Pamela's life was, in almost every respect, the Platonic ideal.

But those events didn't happen, because when Mark shut the car door on his shoelace, he didn't realise until he had to slam on the brakes. As he emerged from his driveway, he spotted an Audi tearing towards him, clearly well over the speed limit. Unfortunately, the shoelace trapped in the door just prevented him from reaching the brake in time, and Mark was killed instantly as the other car smashed into the driver's side door. The fish died a couple of weeks later.

CHAPTER FOUR

What To Do After You Break The Universe

"Come again?"

"They gave me my final warning. One more screw up, they said, and I'm unemployed as well as dead."

"Could be worse. By the way, I would also have accepted the answer 'No, it's mayonnaise this time'"

"Monica Lewinski at the dry cleaners?" "That's the one", you would think that a man with such an encyclopaedic knowledge of bad jokes would have a slightly cheerier attitude to life and what followed. "So what happened?"

"I told 'em they can shove their job where the sun doesn't shine."

"Wow. Get you, Mister Taking Control."

"Well, I have a bit of spare cash - I should be able to get by until something else comes along."

"What you gonna do?"

"Wait 'til I tell you what happened on the last job - I might just have a valuable skill. I might be able to go freelance."

"The Authority aren't going to like that."

"Oh", he screwed his face up, "look, its my trying to care face".

And then Loupe told me the story. Seems to me that walking out of the Authority could be the best thing to happen to him. A lot of people reckon you shouldn't burn your bridges when leaving a job, but I disagree - it's the best thing you can do. You could spend years being one of those schmucks who stays in a job they hate for year after year simply because they lack the proper motivation - and what better motivation for Loupe to get on with his shit than to be in a position where he's unable to buy me drinks? What would he do for conversation then? So, yeah, I always say - go out with a bang and then you're forced to move on to the next thing. Like I say... motivation. Either way, he's OK for now, so we (by which I mean he) get another round. There isn't a problem in the world that can't be solved by applying the proper lubrication, that's my motto. One of my mottoes. It's my motto at the moment. "It means we can get on with getting on, Loupe. We'll make a to-do list to bring forward your therapy schedule. First on the list is making a list - then when we finish the list we can immediately check off the first item on the list - it's a little trick I learned to create an immediate sense of progress."

"Wow, aren't you just the ultimate productivity guru."

"That kind of deadpan sarcasm just doesn't suit you, you know. It makes you look bitter, which adds years to you. It's bad for the complexion." "Like I don't have enough problems."

"You're such a downer - you realise that what you did today is basically impossible, right? You did an impossible thing and you think it's a problem. It says a lot about your bad attitude. You're a glass half empty kind of person, like you're just dragging around your own grubby cloud of woe wherever you go, now me, I'm more of a pragmatist - a glass is twice as big as it needs to be kind of person."

"Spare me."

"Can't, I'm afraid, it's in my contract. I reckon this is the root of all your problems - you are so fucking dismal." He really is - a lot of people hit the afterlife a bit on the depressed side, it's a natural side of effect of a person's demise, but Loupe is something else at times. Misery, woe and sadness. Sprinkles of self-pity. A general malaise, a deep-seated ennui. All in all a deeply miserable bugger, in short. Well, this is all about to change. Tomorrow I'm going to take him out on a little trip - we're going to get to the bottom of his bottomless tragedy, and we'll start with his youth, we'll pay little Loupe a visit, see how things panned out in the playground for him. I guarantee he's not going to like it - they never do, but as they say, you can't make trainers in an empty sweatshop. As for the other thing? I don't know what to make of it - I've never heard of anyone exerting that much pressure on reality from back here, I might just have to put out some feelers, pull in a few of my contacts. Don't think for a second that I'm overstating this - what Loupe did in that house was nothing short of superhuman. Considering he's already classified as a supernatural being, that makes him super-supernatural. "So listen, can you take a few days off? We're going on a field trip tomorrow."

"No problem, they've already insisted that I stay away for a few days to straighten out."

"All the better, 'cause that's exactly what I intend to do."

"And for your next trick, you'll straighten out Liberace? You can't just pray the gay away, you know."

"You can't fix what isn't broken, but you, my old son, are a very different story."

"So where are we going?"

"Somewhere you've been before, a long time ago. We're going to give you the gift of perspective. It's the gift that keeps on giving." In the way that he tends to do, Loupe doesn't reply and lets the conversation trail into a lengthy and awkward silence. It's one of his less appealing features, which is saying something. I really do forget why I like the guy sometimes. Then he calls for more drinks and I remember that I haven't paid for a round in years. There's a lot to be said for a generous drinking partner, even one as frequently dismal as Loupe - and it's not as though he has something better to spend his wages on. As far as I can tell, he has no hobbies, no vices besides the booze, and no real ambitions. He doesn't even chase tail, which is particularly favourite pastime of mine. Get it? Dog joke.

CHAPTER FIVE

The Second Toughest In The Infants'

I suppose in this instance, you could think of me as the ghost of Christmas past - which is probably why Christmas has always given me the willies. Some creepy red suited molester wandering around people's houses judging the behaviour of their kids? It doesn't seem appropriate to sneak in folks' chimneys and cast aspersions on their parenting values, to me. Then leaving gifts for the ones on your "nice" list... that is just plain sinister - I suppose he has "FREE CANDY" spray painted on the side of his sleigh as well - jump in kids, this looks legit.

I always kind of liked A Christmas Carol, though. Rotten old Scrooge with his wicked ways, and then the ghosts - they're a fairly good example of solid psychological techniques for generating change in patients. Examine the past, see how it affects your behaviour in the present, and then extrapolate to the future. If you don't like what that future holds, you can become an agent of change - you've seen how the past affects the present, so logic dictates that the present can affect the future just as much.

The basis of so many people's problems is that they can't see a different path to travel, that their future seems laid out in a thick permanent marker-line of inevitability - once they see their lives in terms of cause and effect, they can start to make positive steps to improve their situation... so we start with me, here, playing the Ghost Of Christmas Past.

Anyway, I digress. Loupe and I start the day on a train, heading to his hometown. Oh yeah, we're heading back to the source, the wellspring from where our dismal little hero began his days. Once we get there, we head to his school to pay him a bit of a visit - figuratively speaking, of course. Places are very powerful things, especially ones that you haven't been to in a long time. Individual bricks, cracks in concrete, bits of decor... any one element of a building can be a key to a memory. The architecture of a building can be a labyrinth containing the keys to parts of the mind that you had completely forgotten existed, until you see a corner that was once a hiding place, or a tiny, forgotten window that you'd once peered through on tiptoes.

I've got to tell you, this school is pretty odd. It's an old victorian schoolhouse build on a very steep road, with concrete playgrounds running up each side. There are markings for playing football, but the playgrounds follow the ascent of the hill the building is on - you can see that for kids playing on there it would lead to a pretty one sided game of football.

Gravity definitely favours the downhill team here. Perhaps they should invent a new game, slalom-ball or something. I can imagine that being the first player facing down the enemy in a game of downhill British Bulldog, it would be seriously intimidating - a simple playground game becoming the start of an ill-matched medieval battle. As for the icy winter months - I'm sure this playground has cracked a lot of young skulls.

Now, time to do my job. I turn to Loupe, and give him the nod, which he reciprocates. Then I pull out my old pocket watch, because I'm nothing if not a hoary old traditionalist, and lead him through a series of deep breathing exercises, trying to get him to relax, to take him down. He watches intently as the watch oscillates back and forth in my paw.

I speak constantly, quietly, words of relaxation and encouragement. I speak of travelling back in time to when he was alive, when he was young, when he was here - and I can see him slipping. I feel myself getting a little woozy myself -

sometimes I'm just too damn talented for my own good. "Sleep now, Loupe, and when you're awake you'll be back here as if you never went away... open up to it, drift down and sleep and travel, and go deeper and down, and down, right to the bottom of your mind...". His eyes are closed, and he's swaying slightly. Job done.

"Now, I'm going to count to three, and on three you're going to wake up and we're going to be back in your youth, so when I get to three I want you to bring yourself back up from the sleep. One. Remember, you're perfectly safe, kiddo. Two. Keep breathing, in and out and in and... three."

Without warning, a bell sounds from within the school, and a riot of children erupts onto the playground from the doors at either end. Loupe's eyes spring open, and he focuses on me. A blink, another, and he looks around. We watch as the student body disgorges itself onto the insane concrete hill. Groups form in the centre, and a ball is magicked out of a bag. Jumpers are thrown into goal post positions, and the ball immediate begins it descent. I was right about that hill. Madness. Other kids take on different games - a group of small kids take assigned positions against a wall near the bottom, and bigger kids take turns kicking a tennis ball at them like some kind of playground firing squad.

"Look", he says, and points to the top of the playground. I follow his finger and squint against the sun.

We can see a young figure hiding under a brick shelter at the top of the hill, skulking behind a large metal post that holds up the roof on the open side of the structure. He's a lank and badly constructed boy, kind of grubby looking, and his trousers look a little on the short side. A funny kid and no mistake, he looks a bit like how I imagine Loupe would have looked at that age. Then I start to notice a few oddities - the clothes around here in general, for a start. They're all wrong - old fashioned. In a playground of well over a hundred kids, there isn't one mobile phone. I start to get a crawling feeling in my fur, and my normally well trained hackles rise.

"That's me."

"Metaphorically speaking, right?"

Wrong.

"No. That's me."

Now, I'm good at this regression stuff, but this is definitely way beyond my abilities. I don't know what's going on with Loupe, but that's his second impossible feat in a week. One more miracle and he could officially qualify for a sainthood. He's dead enough, too. I try to hold down the rising panic, and focus on the situation - we got here when I hypnotised him, so hopefully I can hypnotise us back, or maybe if I just bring him out of the trance. I'll be honest, I'm at a loss.

"Oi, Luke - has your cat died?"

A large boy with a small entourage approaches young Loupe. His role is pretty obvious. Loupe stands next to me, watches impassively as the familiar tale unfolds. Actually, impassive isn't the word. He seems kind of glazed over, lost in a thousand yard stare. I nudge him, but he doesn't respond.

"I said has your cat died?"

Luke demonstrates that he is very much his future dead self's precursor by pointedly ignoring the comment, and looking off into a world of his own. He looks forward with an indifference that anyone older or wiser than our oversized friend would recognise as frightening

- it cloaks him in a shadow that should ward off predators - but this young male isn't yet experienced enough to see it. Ha, I sound like David Attenborough.

"'Cause if not, why are your trousers at half mast!?", he squawks with laughter at his own hilarious joke, and is dutifully joined in chorus by his squeaking band of followers, eager for any scraps of carrion he may leave in his wake. Luke doesn't respond, and our friendly bruiser punches him in the arm, hard. Loupe takes a step forward, as Luke slowly turns to face his would be tormentor. "I remember this little fucker. Matthew Spigot."

"What did you say?" - if I didn't know better, I'd say young Master Spigot somehow heard Loupe, but far more likely is that he's putting words into Luke's mouth to justify the beating he clearly intends to give out. I'm quite sure that in years to come Matthew will be just as concerned with whether or not some innocent bystander called his pint a puff. Either way, Luke isn't buying it, and the big guy takes this as his cue to punch him in the arm again, forcing Luke to take a half a step to the left, deeper into the shadow of the building.

Spigot steps forward again, and this time Luke looks up at him. The shadow on his face deepens, and the tension is like a buzz in the air, a feedback whine. You'll know what I mean if you've ever had a bad accident, or been put under anaesthetic - before the darkness, the world starts to fuzz around you and a rising note overtakes the sounds outside your body. Your consciousness starts to close in on itself and there's a feeling like being compressed.

That's when Loupe rises up behind the boy, reaches forward, grabs Matthews's (admittedly unlikeable) melon head - and bashes it into the metal supporting pole. Just once, but hard enough to leave a dent - and not in the pole. His support squad shrinks back in shock, but Luke simply stands there, impassive, and watches as Spigot slides to the ground, leaving a smear down the pole as he goes.

"What the fuck, Loupe!"

"Funny", he says in a small voice, "I always thought he slipped. You know if we skip forward a year, they'll have demolished this shelter. Everyone just had to get wet after that."

"But! What the fuck, Loupe!"

I can't grab him as such, but I catch his coat in my teeth and drag him away from the scene, leaving Luke stood in his own pillar of darkness as Spigot lies there at his feet and pandemonium starts to unfold in slow motion around them. Away, and down the hill, until the school is out of sight and we take refuge in a park. I sniff the trees nervously, and try to calm down, think happy thoughts. When I've gathered myself, I turn to Loupe, who's sat on the ground by one of the trees, breathing heavily. I walk over to him, and look him in the eye - ready to examine the situation in a calm and rational manner. "What the FUCK, Loupe!?"

"I don't know."

"How did you even do that? That is insane!"

"I know."

"Did you just kill him?"

"I don't know. I suppose so. I know he died. Like I say, everyone assumed he tripped or slipped or had a fit or something." We pause, I try to get it together again. You just can't do this. The dead don't kill the living - those are the rules, the dead can't kill the living - it wouldn't be fair for a start, we outnumber them by a considerable margin, and that's before you factor in other entities that live outside the corporeal plane. Anyway, even if it was possible, which it isn't (or at least shouldn't be) it wouldn't be done because it's just not done. But Loupe went ahead and did it anyway. We're in some serious trouble here, if anyone finds out.

"Listen, Loupe. I thin-"

"He was a bad person, you know."

"Yeah, I'm sure he-"

"Let me tell you something about him."

And Loupe proceeded to tell me a story. When Luke was in his third year at primary school there was a boy who transferred in, called Jacob Pismel, and Luke and Jacob became friends. There was nothing at all wrong with Jacob - he had all of the potential, all the same opportunity as the other kids. He wasn't exceptionally bright, and he wasn't unutterably stupid. His parents were not poor, but nor were they well-to-do. But all of those boys had one thing that Jacob Pismel didn't - a name that didn't easily translate to "Piss-smell".

Matthew Spigot, who as we've already seen was a comic prodigy before his untimely demise, quickly picked up on this, and the name spread like wildfire. It became a self-fulfilling prophecy. Once the joke name stuck, it stopped being a joke. Jacob was ostracised, simply for having an odd name. He became a loner, and started to care less about his hygiene. It didn't take long for him to develop the odour his name attributed to him.

Now here's the really interesting part - once Jacob had taken on the role his name had assigned to him, very soon everyone forgot that the name came before the odour. It was as if it just made sense, that obviously he was called Piss-Smell because of the piss smell. Cause created effect, and then their roles reversed in everyone's mind. It was only right that he was treated with such disdain, only right that everyone called him that, because he deserved it - because it was true. If he didn't like being called Piss-Smell, well he should shower properly, right? Jacob ended up living under a bridge and eating squirrels, probably. If only his name had been Jacob Baker - everyone could have had a nice cake.

"Surely the point of that story is that Jacob was doomed from the start, though?", I told Loupe,

"Surely that's just some kind of parable of inevitability?"

"Maybe so," Loupe replied, "but Spigot started it, and what he started carried on after he died. So maybe what happened today was just as inevitable - after all, it had already happened before I came here and did it, right?"

And with that, Loupe went quiet for a while, and I thought about what he said. I don't like the idea of fate, never have; I'm the master of my own doggy destiny - I fetch my own stick, you might say, and I don't see how I could bother doing anything if everything I was doing was predetermined. But perhaps it works on a different level - if I drop a drink, it's inevitable that it's going to spill... but it wasn't predestined that I was going to drop it. So maybe that's the point - pockets of inevitability caused by previous events, but a wide open world all around them.

Like I'd ever drop a drink, though I'll happily drink a drop.

INTERLUDE TWO

The Almost Untimely Demise Of Pamela Grey

Pamela should have been living a happy and comfortable life with Mark Benson, sharing their delight at their goldfishes' poo trails, but sadly Mark didn't make it to the bowling alley that night, so she never knew the life she'd missed out on. Instead she found herself at a birthday bowling excursion with Rob the IT guy and no actual birthday boy.

Rob the IT guy's Richard Pryor impression was, Pamela had to admit, spot on - though she found something slightly disturbing about a skinny white guy with a slightly lazy eye dropping that many N-bombs. It was a fun night of bowling, though, and she'd not been out at all in far too long - when Rob had suggested she come along, she figured she had nothing to lose. She didn't think she'd meet the love of her life or anything, but it was certainly time to put herself out there again, so she'd fed her fish, put on a nice dress and spent a fun evening rolling some balls. She'd seen Rob again several times after that, and although nothing too serious had come of it, no-one got too badly bent out of shape about it -

and more importantly Pamela had learned that she was ready to get her love life back on track after a couple of years that could be readily described as "a dry spell".

After a few months, she'd got into the swing of being a single girl in the internet age. She'd joined a couple of the popular dating sites and was rapidly starting to turn into a serial dater. Nothing too serious, nothing too intense. She would go for dinner, or for drinks, with all sorts of interesting men from all walks of life. It was rare, though not unheard of, that she would see any of them more than once - what she most enjoyed was the thrill of meeting someone new for the first time. At that point they were all mysteries, puzzles waiting to be unlocked, a reservoir of potential energy waiting to be unleashed. Usually that fizz of possibility had died down by halfway through the first date.

It was November, and Pamela sat down in her favourite armchair with her laptop, a glass of wine sitting beside her. As she did most Thursdays, she logged on to her favourite of the sites she'd joined to see what options she had available. She did pretty well with this site, helped in no small part, she suspected, by the photograph she'd used - in her opinion it struck just the right balance, looking open and friendly but suggesting hidden depths, a touch of mystery. It was one of her favourite photos of herself, which was a rare thing since she usually avoided the lens like the plague. She took a large sip and clicked through into her list of possibilities.

Most weekends she would have a number of potential internet suitors to choose from, and by rolling a dice she'd pick one and enjoy mostly pleasant evenings. That particular weekend she had five options to choose from, so she picked up her lucky dating dice, and gave it a roll. The dice bounced once, twice, and skittered to a halt with three dots pointing up. It was nearly four dots, but as it settled on four an almost imperceptible nudge, a tiny tweak in the fabric of space of time tipped it onto the three, where it rocked slightly before coming completely to rest.

Pamela's life would have changed completely that night, because suitor number four was a very interesting man indeed, by the name of Peter Bellamy. They would have enjoyed a sumptuous dinner at one of the best restaurants in town, where Peter would prove to be the perfect gentleman. Pamela would have been enthralled by his sparkling and effervescent conversation, as she dined on the finest Scottish bouillabaisse with rouille, parmesan and croutons. She would be thrilled by his tales of travels around the world over a culinary soundtrack of ginger and lime marinated trout fillet with caraway seeds. That wasn't to say that Peter would have been a selfish conversationalist, and as they enjoyed their honey and herb panna cotta with a cold berry soup, he would have listened intently as she spoke of her lovely goldfish and her own hopes and dreams.

The wine and the food would all have the desired effect, and in a rare moment of abandon, Pamela chose to throw caution to the wind and go home with her date - something she would never normally do so readily. She considered it fate that she'd worn something appropriate to the situation underneath her dress that night, and as she freshened her make-up in the restaurant bathroom, she was thrilled that someone would get to enjoy it.

Peter's house was a beautiful, secluded detached cottage a few miles outside of the city - set in large gardens. The peace and silence of the place was breathtaking, and compared to the never-ceasing people and traffic noise of the city that she was used to, it was as tranquil as the surface of the moon. Pamela could scarcely believe that it was real. After another couple of glasses of wine, she was more than ready for whatever Peter had to offer, and soon they were kissing their way up the stairs to the immaculate bedroom, a trail of discarded shoes and garments arrayed behind them. Although she wasn't normally into such things, she eagerly played along as Peter blindfolded her and tied her (not too tightly) to the bed. She giggled and he hushed her, said he'd be right back. She didn't mind the anticipation, not one bit.

She listened to him move around the room, wondering what he was doing - she heard a drawer open and close, and then footsteps as he moved back towards the bed. The mattress compressed, rolling her slightly towards him as he climbed on, and she felt his thighs straddle her. Then he leaned forward, and she pushed up from the mattress to meet him as he pressed against her, his breath tickling her ear, his hands running along her arms, testing the restraint of the ties he'd used to fasten her to the bed. He gave them a tug, and when he seemed satisfied that they were secure he eased himself from her again, his weight resting on her abdomen.

His hand reached down to pull the blindfold from her eyes. When Pamela saw that he was wearing another woman's face like some kind of grotesque mask, she managed a number of screams before he could stop laughing hysterically and get around to smashing in her forehead with his hammer, a hammer he'd used on at least seventeen other women he'd found on various dating sites in the last five years.

But those events didn't happen, because Peter Bellamy was number four, and she'd gone for what was behind door number three - which was a chartered accountant named Phillip, who took her to a decidedly average italian place with unimaginative decor and pasta that could only be described as tolerable. He wasn't the worst date of Pamela's reinvented dating life, but he was certainly somewhere in the bottom three, and seemed far more interested in talking about his pet car restoration project than anything that she had any interest in at all, and while she normally would stay polite for the duration of all her dates, she ended up giving him a piece of her mind and storming out. She actually felt much better for the outburst, and returned home feeling a little flushed with power. Life was good, her goldfish persisted, and Pamela happily continued her career as a serial dater.

CHAPTER SIX

*I've Had It With These Motherf**kin' Snakes On
This Motherf**kin' Train*

Normally, I like train travel. There's something
really relaxing about it. You travel by car you
have to deal with thousands of other motorists,
all with their own agendas and their own ideas -
each one a free thinker with the selfish purpose
of getting themselves to their own personal
destination and everyone else can be damned.
Not so on a train, as the rails carry everyone on
board to their destination with a calm certainty
and hypnotic rhythm - we're all travelling in the
same direction here. The nearest thing you might
get to real conflict of interest is when more than
one person needs to use the toilet at the same
time.

That day, well I wasn't feeling it so much. To be
honest, I was more than a little tense, and Loupe
sitting next to me like a ventriloquist's dummy
with no arm up it really wasn't helping matters. I
realise that he'd been through a traumatic
experience and all, but I really hate long
awkward silences.

Of course, the other thing about train travel is that you sometimes get to meet interesting new people, and have conversations you might not otherwise have, widen your view of the world a bit. That's why you should never wear headphones on a train, there's so much to experience in the carriage without locking yourself away from it all. For example, take the thin, pale man who slid himself into the seat opposite us, wearing the Authority shoulder patches and a smile exactly no miles wide. He settled back in the seat, and crossed his hands on the table, appraising us both for an uncomfortable period of time.

"So."

His voice was simply awful, the distillation of every embittered bureaucrat in history, like a blackboard scraping down another blackboard. He paused, and adjusted his tie. I fervently hoped he wasn't going to leave this long a gap between every word he had to say - this train wasn't going to the moon so we were liable to run out of time for smalltalk.

"Mister Loupe. You and your associate here are - and I don't want to understate this - in a lot of trouble. Oh yes, a whole lot of trouble."

Loupe remained silent. I opened my mouth to speak, but the thin man raises a finger and shushes me. I'm not normally one to respond to shushing, but he was very good at it.

"Allow me to introduce myself. My name is Mister Gaunt, and I am your case officer. I realise that may seem strange when you consider that we haven't met at any point, but you'll just have to trust me when I say we prefer to operate in the background. Under the radar, if you will.

"Let's not get into the rather distasteful details of what you've done, Mister Loupe. We're all quite aware of the whole unpleasant situation, and besides, you're not on trial - we can hardly try you for a crime that doesn't exist, now can we? No. Nonetheless, your... situation raises some very interesting questions, and I'm here to take you into what you might want to call... protective custody. I think it's in the interest of both you and your friend here that you both co-operate.

"You see, Mister Loupe, we've been watching you for some time, and the events at the house on your last mission, combined with your atrocious behaviour in the last few hours... well, let's say they explain a few irregularities in our records concerning your birth - and if there's one thing we hate, it's irregularities. Everything we do, Mister Loupe, is to eliminate as many irregularities as possible. We like straight lines, and we like sharp corners. We are working, tirelessly working, to pull some semblance of order out of the boiling maelstrom of reality.

"Have you ever seen the webwork of connections that makes up human existence? It is a knotted and unpleasant thing. Everything is tied to everything else, people are bound together in horribly disordered ways. We are trying to untangle this mess of loops and knots, which is why we do what we do, but sadly our capabilities are limited. A bit of order isn't so much to ask. If you could see how marvellous those strands look when we pull and push and nudge them into line. Beautiful parallel lines of reality, all moving together with a common purpose, people guided into wonderful, solid, dependable destiny. It's glorious - and you seem to be something of a spanner in those works."

Loupe stood up, and mumbled something about the toilet.

"Oh, do feel free - though you should be aware that this train won't be stopping until we get to our destination. There's nowhere for you and your friend to run, Mister Loupe. There's nowhere for you to hide, so yes, feel free. Take your time."

Loupe wandered off down the carriage, and I heard the door slide shut behind him. I faced Gaunt, who looked at me like an insect - both in the sense of "as if I were an insect" and "like an insect looks at another thing, possibly a smaller insect".

"Listen, Gaunt, I don't know what you think you're doing, but Loupe is my client, and I don't think you have his welfare as your top priority."

"Oh you're right. In fact I would say it's roughly ninth on the list. Making sure our uniforms are nicely pressed is probably a higher priority than Mister Loupe's welfare."

"Well what makes you think I'll let you get away with it?"

"A good question. What makes you think you can do anything about it?"

"I'm a licensed therapist, for one. I have connections."

"Oh, connections. Well that's perfectly frightening. Of course, connections are only really any use if you can actually connect with them, aren't they? Perhaps if you had some legal right to a phone call, for example. Which you do. You have plenty of legal rights.", he smiled a predatory smile, "but that doesn't mean we're necessarily going to give you your legal rights. You see, rights are always entirely dependent on the willingness of those in control of a given situation to provide those rights. In other words - a right is not necessarily a given. Do you follow?"

It was at that point I realised just how big a pile of freshly deposited trouble we were in. When it came to taking prisoners, Gaunt clearly wasn't taking any prisoners, and things were clearly going Guantanamo really fast. Or you might say Gaunt-anamo.

"Your friend is taking his time."

"Well, maybe it's a number two. We had a big meal before we caught the train."

"You have a big mouth."

"Well, I'm a dog - it's a natural part of our physiognomy. I'd say you humans have really small mouths, must be murder catching a ball."

"Yes. You're a funny little pooch, aren't you? Nonetheless - may I be candid? - you might want to consider putting a sock in it, or I'll cut your tongue out. Wait here."

I considered putting a sock in it, and on consideration considered it to be a considerably better idea than to keep talking. Gaunt stood up, spidered his way out of the narrow seat and set off down the aisle, his spindly legs creaking. The carriage door hissed open, and then hissed shut. Silence, followed by quite a bit more silence. Then the carriage door hissed open again, and I heard Gaunt's footsteps clattering up the aisle once more. A bony hand reached over the seat and grabbed my scruff, pulling me upright. Nose to nose, and eye to eye, Gaunt fixed me in a furious stare, and I knew immediately that Loupe had pulled a fast one. Good for him. I've not met many people like Gaunt, but I've met enough to know that people like him get right up my nose. I give my biggest, bestest, baddest breathiest smile.

"If you're going to kiss me, Gaunt, you could at least pretty yourself up first. Maybe put on a nice dress."

"Kiss you?", screamed Gaunt as he turned a rather fetching purple hue, "If you don't tell me where that little bastard's gone I'm going to fuck you like you've never been fucked before."

CHAPTER SEVEN

Putting The Past In Front Of You

I felt bad for leaving JuJu back there, but I don't think I really had a choice. Besides, I was the one Gaunt was after. I was feeling pretty strange at that moment - like something was waking up inside me, a muscle I never knew I had. More than that, entire limbs - tentacles of power that plug directly into the machinery of the universe. I found myself wondering what else I could do, how far I could go.

Of course, first things first, you're probably wondering how I made my astonishing escape. Now that was pretty simple - most things are easier to do once you've done them once, when you have the trick of them. I just reached out with one of those tentacles and... twist, just so. The train was moving, so it wasn't there five minutes from now, but I was - if you follow my meaning. Sadly I was several feet above the tracks, and I'm very lucky there wasn't another on the route, but you take the rough with the smooth. As landings go, it was on the rough end of the spectrum, though.

I picked myself up, and dragged myself to the edge of the rails, where I took a breather. I was going to have a long walk back home. It was dark by the time I arrived at the old Central station, and it took a good couple of hours more to get back to the school. From there, it was just ten more minutes to my parents' house - well, where my parents' house used to be. There was none of it left now, new houses had grown from what was left - shiny monstrosities with awful pale bricks, each front door the same - a homogenous estate for people who merely existed in their houses, rather than living in their homes.

I flexed that muscle again, and could feel the time washing over me like a warm wind, faster and brighter as I pushed harder, as hard as I could. If it helps, you can imagine it like The Time Machine, the new buildings clattering down and the old one flaring into life like an old Lego advert, the sun unrising and unsetting faster and brighter. Of course, it wasn't like that - it was more like pushing against a membrane, and then it sphinctered open and I just... popped through, into then. The house was newer than I remembered it. The door looked newly painted - the same green I remember, but brighter and fresher. The lawn was better kept, and the windows cleaner. When I was young, the house was gloomy, dark - a lonely place carpeted with regret. This house, while clearly the same house, had been refitted with hope and vigour. I never saw it like this, so I figured this must be before I was born. I crept up to the door.

It took me several minutes and a not inconsiderable number of false starts before I could bring myself to go in, and the riot of colour inside took my breath away. For a moment I thought I must have come to the wrong place - the rooms were decorated in bold strokes, each one like some kind of celebration. It was only the presence of familiar items that made me believe this was my parents' house - the picture of my grandmother - Nan, my mother's mother, sitting proudly on the wall in a ridiculously overblown gilt frame. That picture hung there my whole life, and my dad always said how much she looked like my mum. Based on the pictures of her and my own memories, I think he was right.

Into the kitchen, and time stood still, as if holding its breath. Not through any manipulation of mine, though. There she was, sat at the kitchen table, reading a magazine in the afternoon sunlight. Just as she was, just as she would always be in my memories, except for the slight rise of her belly as I was taking shape inside her. I'd like to be able to describe the feeling in romantic terms, to describe the rush of adrenaline, the elevation - but that's not really how it was. I burst into tears and nearly threw up. Of course, she didn't hear me, she couldn't hear me - and she laughed at something in the magazine. I found myself thinking how odd it was that she would laugh out loud when she was by herself. How odd it was that she should laugh at all. I don't remember her ever doing that.

You see, this is a scene that wouldn't last forever. She was never like this after I was born - some darkness took her over. She loved me well enough at first, I suppose, but there was something wrong - like I'd taken something from her, or ruined something. I don't think she hated me for it, it was like I was a bad dog who'd made a mess of the carpet - I simply didn't know any better. It got worse though, and she would fall into terrible rages, or black moods that lasted for days at a time. She would sit in that chair in the kitchen, in the dark, just sitting there. And she didn't laugh, not once.

My memories are scattered - a bottle of milk shattering against the wall, and the following sour smell that didn't go away for a very long time. Her beating her fist against the curtains in the living room, screaming "Oh yes! Unclean!

Unclean!" in some make-believe leprosy. I didn't know the word for it back then, but she was spiralling, and I knew that something was very wrong with her, and it didn't take long to learn that I couldn't help, and I was best served by staying as far away as I could. And she didn't laugh, not once.

I remember when I lay there in my bed and she just leaned in over me and screamed and screamed, incomprehensible words, just pouring out of her like drunken vomit - the devil speaking in tongues. I remember when she bashed her head on the toilet, and when she did it again to make sure until she was unconscious. I remember when she drank the washing up liquid and foam spewed out of her mouth like some kind of rabid animal. I remember when she drank the bleach and the ambulance had to come and take her to the hospital. And she didn't laugh, not once.

I remember the bewilderment when my dad told me that wouldn't be coming back, with his red ringed eyes and a mask of grief and relief. She was never coming back, he said. And we went to the building with the box in it, and she was in the box (but she wasn't in the box, he said), and the man in the dress sent the box away and in all that time she didn't laugh. Not once.

After that, my dad kind of closed down. He was always there, but he was rarely present - and I learned to be still, to be quiet. The day Matthew Spigot died, when he just slipped in the playground and dashed his head open so you could see his brains, I came home in tears, horrified. He told me that the world was cruel like that. He told me I should get used to it. I learned to keep it all to myself.

A few times, I found notes that he'd written. I called them goodbye notes. I was terrified he was going to leave. Of course, they were more than that, though in the end it was smoking in bed that got him - got him, and the house, and all of the pictures on the walls, and all of the photos in the box in the pantry. It nearly got me too, but I threw blankets and pillows out of the window and jumped out onto them like they showed me on the TV, and I had a front row seat as the house burned to the ground, and I watched it burn until the firemen took me away.

And yet here she was, sat at the old kitchen table, reading a magazine and laughing, and she looked up as the front door opened, and I heard my dad walking in and shouting a hello, the whole setup like some dream advert for better domestic living. She was smiling and he kissed her, and he touched her belly with me in there -

and for just a minute I forgot everything that came after, everything that had gone before, because we looked like a family, even though I hadn't even been born yet.

INTERLUDE THREE

The Unhealthy Obsession Of Phillip Stokes

Phillip kicked Clarissa in the side, hard. He was furious - the bitch had cost him thousands and thousands and had brought him nothing but disappointment. Of course, she just sat there and took it, like she always did - sullen and uncomplaining, yet always demanding more of him. What did he get for all his effort? Abuse. He wasn't appreciated by anyone. He kicked her again, harder this time. What more did she want from him? Blood? He'd have done it if he'd thought it would help, would have opened a vein if that was what it took - and she'd have soaked it up like a sponge, the ungrateful whore. He lashed out one more time as she squatted there, comatose and unresponsive, and connected - hard. Then her wing mirror fell off.

He'd never been angry at her like this before - he'd doted on her, given her everything she needed, and always the best of the best. The finest oil, each part carefully polished to a pristine shine before being replaced. He'd had her upholstery redone in sumptuous moleskin, and hand crafted new walnut panels for the dashboard, sandpapering and polishing until his hands were raw. So what had changed? It was that woman the other night. They'd just been going for dinner, he'd not even tried one of those dating sites before, but one of his friends had badgered him into trying it. She'd just been so mean about Clarissa, about him. Said he was self-absorbed and obsessive, said that he needed to "get a life".

Who was she to call him a loser? He bet she was a regular on those sites, so it hardly seemed fair that she should be able to judge him like that. Still... it had stung, and stuck to him like a cloud of flies since, and now he was taking it out on the one girl who'd never let him down - and look what had happened. He picked up the wing mirror, which fortunately hadn't cracked, but suffered some slight scuffing. He reached for the polish and chamois leather, and got to work bringing it back to perfection, before fitting it back on to Clarissa. He muttered to himself as he did so, apologising for his outburst - it wasn't her fault, he said, promising it would never happen again.

Once his work was done, he sat in the drivers seat, and made the decision that today would be the day - Clarissa might not be entirely ready, but she was more than good enough to make her debut. He reached for the key and fired her up, and oh how she purred. It was like she was telling him she forgave him for his temper, that none of it mattered now... they could go out on the town together because nobody else's opinion mattered - she would always be his girl. He thumbed the remote for the garage door, and it swivelled open, revealing a crisp and bright winter's day outside. A perfect day for a man to put on his best calfskin driving gloves and go for a drive with the top down, and his scarf flying behind him.

He pulled out into the street, and the road unrolled before him like a red carpet for a dignitary at the ambassador's party. Head held high, he turned right, and headed for the country - he could tell people were casting admiring looks his way as he cruised through the streets of the city, and rightly so, Clarissa was a beauty that any man would be proud to have on his arm. Soon, the streets became suburban, and then he found himself on open country roads - much more secluded so he and Clarissa could get a little more intimate. He opened up her throttle and she growled with pleasure.

A momentary distraction, as Clarissa's glove box popped open, as if some mysterious force had given the catch a quick tug, and Phillip took his eyes off the road, and in those few seconds when his attention was diverted, his life was changed irrevocably.

What should have happened is this - he should have seen the hitchhiker in the road, her dog walking faithfully by her side, and he should have slowed down to pass. He wouldn't have picked her up - imagine allowing a dog on this upholstery, but he could have continued happily on his way, enjoying Clarissa's first day out as he should have, stopping at a country pub for a delicious home-cooked meal and perhaps a cheeky half a mild. It would have been the perfect day. The other patrons in the pub would have eyed up Clarissa admiringly, maybe even with a touch of envy, and he would sit, revelling in the fact that she was all his.

Unfortunately, that wasn't how it all panned out.

He looked up from the flipped glove box to see Jenni Mullen, the hitchhiker and her dog, who's name was Gordon just too late to do anything about it. Gordon took the worst of the impact as he slammed on Clarissa's brakes, and the poor animal was smashed against the radiator hard enough to dent it. Fur and blood and other fragments flew, smearing up the bonnet and windscreen.

Jenni was winged by the Clarissa's front corner, the impact taking out her right knee and pretty much destroying her fibia and tibula, as well as most of the bottom of her femur. She span and flew in a way that in other circumstance might be considered gymnastic before gravity unceremoniously dumped her in a ditch, her head impacting against a rock, knocking her out cold.

Clarissa left a long trail of rubber on the road before coming to a halt. Phillip sat in the car, breathing heavily, adrenalin coursing through his veins, his mind buzzing with terror. He hit the switch for her hazard lights, and leapt from the car and ran back to where Gordon's pulped body lay in the road. His nerves screaming, he ran over to the ditch where Jenni's body lay. Blood oozed from a cut on her temple, soaking the rock that had become her pillow, and her leg lay at several angles a leg shouldn't lay at, a piece of bone protruding from her ruined shin.

He reached for his mobile phone, and then looked at the girl lying in the ditch. Crunch time. He looked back up the road at Clarissa, and made his choice. He ran to the car and got in, giving one last glance over his shoulder before driving home as fast as he could, praying the police wouldn't stop him for the state of his radiator. Fortunately, he made it, and drove her straight into the garage, the door swinging shut behind him.

It didn't matter how hard he scrubbed, how many layers of polish and wax - even when the dent was gone, Clarissa just wasn't the same. He could still see the stains on her, and every time he even smelled the expensive moleskin upholstery his mind returned to the girl in the ditch, the girl he left for dead. Even when he covered Clarissa in a thick tarpaulin, and stopped going to the garage at all - as he drifted to fitful sleep at night he'd imagine he could hear the clicking of the relay that controlled her hazard lights. Six months later, hollow eyed and sleepless, he drove her to the old quarry with the deep pool at the bottom.

CHAPTER EIGHT

Magnesium Sulphate

This new ability of mine was getting pretty easy to use now, though it became apparent there were limits. I tried to go back further, but it seemed like there was some kind of barrier - I stuck around the old homestead, and tried to push, but found I couldn't go anywhen before the point of my conception. Before you ask, no, I didn't check that particular magic moment out, that would be a level of voyeurism that no sane man could recover from. So it appeared I had become some kind of latter-day Sam Beckett. Of course this raised more questions than that - how far forward could I go? How much of what happens to me could I see, and if I see something I don't like... can I change it?

I kept skipping forwards, watching as my parents approached my birth. The bag was packed, everything was ready to go, and finally the time came. There was excitement, panic, a flurry of activity... and that was when it all started to go wrong. I saw the doctor talking to my dad - he said it was pre-eclampsia - something to do with blood pressure, a dangerous surge of hypertension. The little me was struggling to get out of there when my mother's seizures began. The doctors quickly bundled my dad out of the room, and turned back to her.

Magnesium Sulphate - a.k.a. Epsom Salts, apparently this stuff was just the ticket, and they threw some into her veins as fast as they could. I stood and watched as she screamed that it burned inside her, that it was like fire in her blood, as the chemicals frothed around her system. They checked the pressure again, and upped the dose. This was the mother I knew though, as she raved in that bed - driven outside of reality, her arteries twitching with columns of marching fire ants. Something told me this was the first time that demented light had appeared in her eyes, the first time her brain started to go sideways.

This continued for a couple of hours, and each time they seemed to get it under control the whole cycle would begin again. My father came in and out of the room, looking overwhelmed and terrified. Finally they brought in a consultant, and they brought in an anaesthesiologist, and the decision was made to perform an emergency caesarian section - so I was to be cut from my mother's belly like a tumour. From my mother's womb untimely ripped, is that it? Of course, I knew this, but it was a whole different ball game seeing it happen rather than just knowing it had happened.

I can tell you this - an operating room in the 1970s was not the wondrous cave of technology you'll see today. It seemed terribly basic to me - I imagined that if these surgeons and nurses were thrown into a victorian operating theatre they'd think much the same thing. It almost looked barbaric, but nonetheless they took her down and they draped her and the surgeon stepped in and cut her open.

As the incision was made, I saw the first wisps of smoke rising from the wound. Clearly I was the only one here who could see it, as the medical team carried on regardless - opening her up, releasing a curling shadow. It boiled over her skin like a dark dry ice, coiled up the arms of the surgeon as he did his work. Then he reached in and pulled me from the door he'd cut for me, and the proto-me was released into the light. I looked rubbery, grey, malformed - and the shadow was stuck to me as if by some kind of static electricity - I could see it coiling down the umbilical cord, strands of it sticking to the edges of the wound and stretching to my newborn body.

Then they cut the cord, and for the first time we were two separate creatures. The shadow coiled around me as the midwife let rip with the classic refrain of "It's a beautiful baby boy" - but my father wasn't there to hear, and my mother was lost in the abyss of general anaesthesia. Then the little me opened his mouth and bellowed his distaste at the whole inhumane affair. The midwife bundled me off to be weighed and measured, wrapped in a blanket, and placed in one of many cots in one of those Orwellian nurseries.

I followed myself on my journey, and stood next to my dad, peering through the window as I lay there under my blue blanket - small and red, with bits of that shadow still sticking to me. I turned to him, and wanted to say something, but there was nothing I could say that he would hear. I wondered how what he felt related to what I felt - I suppose there is no analogue - countless men have felt the combination of terror and pride as they see their newborn for the first time, but how many find themselves in the bizarre situation of witnessing their own birth?

There was another look on my dad's face though - as well as the pride and the relief, something I couldn't put my finger on. A shifty look, a guilty look. As he watched me sleep, he would periodically look over his shoulder, or quickly peer left and right from his reflection in the glass. It was almost as if he was expecting someone to be stood behind him - like he'd said Candyman at the mirror too many times and was starting to regret it, you know, just in case. If only he knew that the future ghost of his dead son was stood right next to him.

I noticed that none of the other babies in the nursery had that sticky, dark candy floss gathering in wisps around them - a darkness that I believe followed me through my whole corporeal life. Even now though, it was growing thinner - creeping inside me where it would stay, coiled up like a tapeworm. I don't know how I knew, but this thing fed on me - it was a parasite and I was both its keeper and its sustenance. Every day of my life I would live with it, and it would be the source of my fears. It would watch my mother decline and grow stronger as she did.

Whatever else that shadow was, I was convinced that it was the poison that had ruined my life, and it was the remedy that stopped it from killing me. Maybe it was even the smell of it that brought the being that would kill my own son into my sphere - maybe that entity was even now spiralling in ever shrinking circles, a decaying orbit that would collide in another nursery years from now. If so, I had no inkling of where it was, or what it was - I didn't have the tools or the wherewithal to fight it, but maybe I could find that somewhere. For the first time, I considered the possibility that what had gone so wrong was maybe not so inevitable after all.

CHAPTER NINE

The Unfortunate Victim Of An Extraordinary Rendition

"Wow, nice place you have here, guys. Did you decorate it yourself? I hear the torture porn dungeon cum brutalist office space look is going to be very big in the spring, so you're well ahead of the curve."

I had no idea where Loupe had got to, and I was fervently hoping he hadn't forgotten about me, in the meantime my natural ability to wag my tongue instead of my tail was getting me in hot water with my captors, who it appears had been subject to a cruel series of humourectomy experiments.

To be honest. we'd got off to a bad start as they discovered how hard it is to tie a dog to a chair designed for restraining humans - that managed to put them in a bad mood from the off, so everyone seemed to be feeling a bit punchy, as the first of Gaunt's friendly associates (whom I dubbed Huey) was keen to demonstrate, with a reasonably offensive left hook to my very sensitive snout. He maybe should have warned

Dewey though, who got the worst of the resulting saliva spray. I shook my head to clear the stars and cartoon birds.

"That's a good hook. Though as a trained therapist, I have to tell you that studies show these kind of tough love methods really aren't an effective motivator. Also, I think you've maybe been watching the wrong movies, 'cause there's no such thing as bad cop, bad cop, and another bad cop. Can I have my phone ca-"

It turns out Huey's right hook was equally impressive, and this time Louie bore the spittly brunt of it. The door behind my new friends clacked open, and in strode Gaunt, his face impassive. He pulled up a metal chair, you know the kind, and spun it round to sit facing me, his arms folded over the back of it. What a cliche.

"Where's Loupe?"

"Don't know. Wouldn't tell you if I did. A dog has standards."

"You realise that he presents a clear danger to himself, and to our whole way of life, don't you?"

"I think the word you're looking for is afterlife, and I'm willing to bet that he presents more danger to your particular status quo more than any kind of ominous peril to the universe as we know it."

"Let me put it another way, perhaps in terms you will understand. If a dog has rabies, it must be put down, for the good of everybody else. That's what Loupe is - he's sick, and his particular brand of sickness could infect everyone and everything around him."

"Oh no! Loupe has rabies? We shared a glass the other day! Do you think I might have it, sir?"

"Ha. Loupe's sickness is more subtle than that - Loupe's sickness is chaos. He's not aware of it but he could undo the work of centuries."

"No, Loupe's sickness is choice, and I think it's possible that if you're still beating up folks in grotty rooms after hundreds of years, perhaps your work is due a bit of undoing."

Gaunt pauses, sits upright, his hands grasping the sides of the chair. He must realise he's not going to get anything out of me - if there's one thing that everybody knows about man's best friend, it's that we're loyal to the last. He must have heard of that little mutt in Scotland who sat on his master's grave until he died. The dog, I mean. The master was already dead, hence the grave.

"Perhaps we're going about this all wrong. I can see how our approach to the whole Loupe problem may have given you the mistaken impression that we're the bad guys. Certainly the way we've treated you could possibly lead you to that conclusion. Maybe we all need to take a short time-out and cool down a little. But I need you to understand, we aren't the bad guys by any means - we're the good guys, we're the efficient guys. It's true that our methods can sometimes seem a little coarse, brutal even - but in an organisation this size, we are naturally inclined toward the most effective route to the results we require - and you'd be amazed at how effective these methods can be."

I declined to justify his continued mouth-noise with an answer. It's a well established fact that if there are two groups of people in conflict, and Group A is the group with the uniforms and the shiny boots, and if they wear their uniforms and shiny boots to protracted sessions of trying to beat information out of Group B... well they're clearly the bad guys. Naturally, they don't like to admit it - your average Nazi didn't dance to work singing the "hooray for being evil" song, but it's still fairly black and white. Gaunt gestured to the door, and Huey, Dewey and Louie trooped out dutifully.

"Anyway, clearly we're not going to persuade you to help us like this, so it's time, I think, to put down the stick, and offer the carrot instead."

"Delightful, squire. You are going to lube it up first, right?"

"Yes, very good. Ha ha.", he didn't laugh, he just said the word ha twice, "But the carrot I refer to is purely financial. You are a freelancer, are you not? A businessman."

"Business-dog." He ignored me.

" So perhaps money is the language you really understand? We would be willing to provide you with a considerable reward if you were to reconsider your allegiances. The Authority can be very generous when needs must, when generosity is the most efficient solution."

"You're having a laugh, right? Can we just get the jolly team of triplets back in and get back to the vigorous beating? It has to be preferable to listening to you talk."

"How much do you owe now? According to our records, you're well behind on your Deadbeat card, and in the hole with people considerably less charitable than us when it comes to the crunch.", he relished the word "crunch" a little too much, if you ask me.

"I get by, thanks, always have done, always will."

"Well let's see how you get by when we giftwrap you and leave you on The Mouse's doorstep, shall we? Let's see how you get by then."

I did my best sullen face, as he paused. He pinched a small piece of lint from the lapel of his jacket, and inspected it, before placing it in his breast pocket and prissily patting the flap down. He straightened, and stood, turning towards the door. As he was about to leave the room, he turned back to me.

"I have been authorised to offer you two million."

Now, hold on a cotton-pickin' minute there, don't you go judging me. It's easy to sit on your high horse when you haven't spent the last few hours being beaten silly by Donald Duck's psychotic nephews, and Gaunt was right - I owed money to some pretty shady shades. I'd already told you that Loupe was a bit of a dick, and think about it - he bashed a kid's head in on a steel pillar. You just shouldn't do that in front of your friends, it ends up putting them in really difficult, ethically challenging situations. It's a good a job I got my City and Guilds in Moral Dilemma Management. The fact is, just like everyone else - I'd rather be the sticker than the stuck, and I'll choose being the sickness over being sick.

"Bullshit, you're authorised to offer at least twice that. Where do you think I was born, on a weetabix farm? Now we can haggle all day or you can just skip to the maximum and we can talk, man to dog - and what does a hound have to do to get a drink and some kibble round here?"

Gaunt smiled that awful, predatory not-really-a-smile-actually. Closing the door again, he returned to the chair and faced me, steepling his fingers together like every evil cliche in the book. If he'd had a moustache he would surely have given it a dramatic twirl as his top hat loomed over his forehead.

"Three million."

I'm not proud of it, but I would have settled for the two.

INTERLUDE FOUR

The Difficult Recovery Of Jenni Mullen

It was actually Gordon who saved her life, even though he was dead. Lots of motorists passed his corpse by, but finally someone saw his remains in the road, and noticed that the he was still wearing his collar and lead. The implications of this sank in further along the road, and the man immediately turned back to investigate. Jenni was still unconscious when he found her, and remained that way when the police and ambulance turned up.

That she survived, they told her later, was a miracle. She was incredibly lucky to be alive. She asked for more morphine, due to the unbearable pain in her leg. That was when the nurses looked uncomfortable, and called for the doctor. She sat down with Jenni and gently explained to her what had happened, that despite the best efforts of the paramedics, and then the medical team, her leg was beyond salvation. They'd had to amputate. As she spoke, Jenni felt like the doctor's voice was coming to her from the end of a rapidly extending tube, and overlaid with rising feedback, a buzzing in her skull.

Reality drifted further away, and then she suddenly snapped back to the material plane. Everything came sharply into focus, and she could finally see how the sheets sat all wrong. She resisted the urge to lift the blanket and look. The longer she could leave it before she saw it, the longer it wouldn't be true. She asked the doctor about Gordon.

Oddly, she was more upset by her dog's death than the loss of her leg. Gordon had travelled with her all over the country, and had helped her make friends. He was a good natured hound, with a real knack of breaking the ice with strangers. He'd known a few tricks that always got people on side, and seemed to instinctively know which ones to use when. On the few occasions when she'd had to sleep rough, he'd kept her warm. When she found herself sleeping in a strange place where perhaps things felt a little unsafe, he'd stood guard. Now Gordon was gone, and her leg was gone.

After a few days in hospital, the subject of contacting her family came up. She didn't want to, but really she had no choice. Phone calls were made, and when she was discharged, her parents came to pick her up, taking her back to the house she'd left all those years ago to begin her physical therapy. They loaded up with pamphlets about stump care and prosthetics, and they all pretended she'd never gone away.

Jenni wasn't wired for this kind of life though - she liked to be on the road, to keep moving, and being stuck in one place started to make her mind go a bit sideways. Combined with the rigorous physiotherapy and the general challenges of recuperation, she became insular and angry - her parents tried to be patient but one too many meals thrown at the wall started to take their toll. She was left to her own devices more often, as her company became increasingly unbearable.

Listening to her parents' car start in the drive and then disappear into the distance, going anywhere to get away from her for a few hours, Jenni prepared to take her own journey. She certainly wasn't short of powerful painkillers. She didn't bother to write a note - this wasn't some cry for help, as far as Jenni was concerned it was just time to move on. Time to hit the road again. The best thing, she thought, was that this was so easy. Twenty-five dihydrocodeine, all in a row. One at a time, down the hatch - she did it like she would eat smarties when she was a kid, after lining them up, she'd take one from one end of the row, and then one from the other until they were all gone. Then she lay back on her pillow and felt a pleasant numbness start to wash over her. It was good stuff, this.

If some mysterious and intangible force hadn't pushed her mother's purse out of sight, then she would have got away with it - dizziness would have started to spin her around, and through shortening breath she would have slipped into a sleep from which she would never wake, at least not in this reality. Her story would have been shortened to a simple paragraph ending with a self-induced full stop.

Instead, through the rising nausea, she heard her parents' car returning to the gravel drive, and her mother's footsteps, a key in the lock. Her mother clattered about, searching for her missing purse, finding it behind a picture of Jenni when she was very small. It doesn't take much to remind you of what's important to you, and seeing the picture gave Valerie pause. Jenni was slipping away into a chemically induced sleep as Valerie walked up the stairs to check on her daughter, to say they'd be back soon.

Jenni cursed, realising her plans were ruined, but was too far gone to do anything about it. Valerie pushed the door open, intending to just peep around and say a quick goodbye, but some instinct made her walk all the way into the room instead. She didn't know how she could tell something was wrong, perhaps some kind of parents' instinct, but then she saw the empty blister packs on the bedside table - blister packs she'd been keeping tidy despite Jenni's rage and lack of gratitude.

The paramedics arrived quickly, but still Jenni was unconscious. She didn't respond as Valerie shook her, was like a rag doll as Valerie shouted at her to wake up. Her pupils were contracted so small they were barely there. The medics rushed into the room and quickly administered a drug called Naloxone, blocking the further passage of opiates into Jenni's brain. To Valerie, it seemed almost like a miracle as Jenni started to breathe again, and opened her eyes. She hadn't wanted this second chance, she hadn't asked for it, but she'd got it anyway - and things were going to be different.

CHAPTER TEN

My My My, Eliza

The Skeleton Key was something of a legend amongst those who frequented it. In the time I used to go there, it closed down at least three times, changed owners countless times, and always steadfastly resisted any attempt to change it, to bring it upmarket, even just to clean it up. The bar was scratched to all hell and too short to serve the number of patrons who generally partook at it - and the eternal presence of barflies who insisted on taking up seated residence at that undersized booze runway didn't help matters. If you could battle your way through the throng, and squeeze past the strange old men with their Guinness and oversized elbows, though, at least you were always guaranteed slow and surly service.

There was a stage, and pretty much every weekend was taken with the thrashing noise of bands from the area, everything from flopheaded teens who'd just discovered Joy Division and really taken the whole thing to heart, to bearded twenty-somethings with that creative spark who were old enough to know better and young enough to not care, to even older wannabees who really should just have known better.

If you've never been involved in a scene like that, I can tell you that it's a strange combination of the deadly serious and utterly ridiculous. Everybody wants to think they have the potential to be the next big thing, and the hipsters act all studiously unimpressed. It doesn't matter though, because most of the bands just give up in the end, and there are always more like them ready to slot into the vacuum they leave. Because of this constant turnaround of failure built on other failure, The Skeleton Key persisted.

The toilets were a shocking state, but it had become de rigeur for everyone who played there, local acts or out-of-towners to leave their mark. The walls had been painted once, but every square inch was scribbled and scratched with the names and logos of aspiring music legends of every stripe, as well as messages to and disparagements about pretty much every one of the Key's regulars. You could regularly expect some kind of lock-in, if you'd paid your dues with attendance at gigs good and gigs bad - at which point the secret ashtrays would appear as if by magic and the smoking ban would be recklessly ignored by the clustered die-hards as they threw down an extra few pints, shots, or both.

There were a lot of good times to be had in this hallowed hall, and a lot of good memories. I never got up on that stage myself (except in one memorable final showdown of a Wednesday night quiz, where knowing the American word for "truncheon" brought in a prize of yet more drink for our already sodden heads), and was always more of an appreciator/sarcastic mocker depending on the quality of the act. I made a lot of good friends, had a lot of drunken adventures, and most importantly, the Skeleton Key is where I met Eliza.

That night, however, I was having one of those miserable nights - didn't want to stay out, didn't want to go home, didn't want another drink, didn't want to sober up. The band that were playing at the time were pushing all the wrong buttons - so I'd gone out to the beer garden for a smoke, and was just lurking in the bad corner, sinking into a shadow both real and figurative. We've all had nights like it, when someone needs to make sure our mobile phone is taken away from us, and our internet access has a breathalyzer on it to keep our keyboard locked for the safety of ourselves and others. Everyone else was inside watching the band, and I really couldn't understand why - I can't remember exactly what they were like, or what they were called, but I was glad to be outside where their awful noise was muffled away.

Then Eliza wandered out into the beer garden with her friend, and they sat down, lit up cigarettes and started making jokes about how bad the band were. I stayed in my shadow and earwigged, and I can't tell you how pleased I was - I'd honestly been starting to believe that I must be the only person in the whole place with no taste, but listening to Eliza and her friend, I realised that we were the only three people in the joint with taste. On that night, at least.

So that was the first emotion that Eliza ever made me feel, before I even knew her name, before I'd even spoken to her, before she'd even set eyes on me... she made me feel relieved. That may seem like a strange starting point for what could be rightly classified as a Great Romance, but there it was, and despite it being an odd first emotional step, I can't tell you how much I enjoyed that feeling. They were lighting their second smokes, but were having trouble with the lighter. So I stepped out of my shadow, and took the opportunity to say hello by offering them a light.

At which point she looked at me like I was a mental case.

Nonetheless, after several weeks of bumping into each other at the bar, in the beer garden, and on one rather embarrassing occasion in the ladies toilets (long story, I can tell you that the ladies had considerably less graffiti than the gents), we ended up having actual conversations, some of which I was sober enough to not make myself look like a total idiot in. Really though, it was all getting a bit Hugh Grant (as in I was being a romantic comedy buffoon, nothing to do with transvestite hookers), and I was clearly in danger of being relegated to the Friend Zone, so I took the plunge, and asked her out on a date.

At which point she looked at me like I was a mental case, again, and said she'd think about it.

Let me describe her to you - she was kind of average height, with hair the colour of strained peaches - she used to dye it back then, and it was just coming out of an orange phase, like that girl in that movie, you know the one I mean. She would talk chiefly with her hands, and often nearly knocked peoples glasses off, or drinks out of their hands, or burned herself on passing cigarettes. Her dress sense was eclectic, to say the least, which kind of reflected her fickle sense of mischief. I remember one of the first things I noticed about her were her teeth, her mouth in general - she had a sparkling smile, and perfect teeth, and always wore really bright red lipstick - a shade not many women could pull off, but believe me she did.

So we went on that date, and most of the time she looked at me like I was a mental case, and fortunately for me it was the first of many - Eliza turned out to be the antidote to that sticky shadow, a shaft of sunlight that I could bask in and forget the black dog that was following me. Time passed, and somehow she didn't grow bored of me, even seeming to find whatever she saw charming.

Step by step we went through the milestones of all big relationships. We had arguments, and we made up. We reached the point of having toothbrushes and spare underwear at each other's houses. From there it was a short step to actually moving in together, and trying to work out how to fit two people's lives into a space that previously only contained one. I learned the art of compromise, also known as "throwing my stuff away", but I didn't really mind - she had far better taste than I did.

It was our second christmas of living together when I popped the question - which always struck me as a very trite phrase for what I considered to be a Neil Armstrong level step. "Popped the question" - it conveys so little of the excitement and blistering terror of asking someone to spend the rest of their life with you. Sure, the statistics suggest that won't be the case, but you can prove anything with statistics.

You're not asking someone to be with you until you get bored, or until one of you fucks up - you're asking them to be with you forever. So someone really should come up with a better way of explaining it than "popping the question". I did it as properly as I could, and even went down on one knee, because that's what you're supposed to do - it actually helps, that one move, that drop to one knee (as long as you're not tying your shoelace) asks the question for you. I think then our stammering through the question itself only serves to provide thinking time, and fills in what would otherwise be a very uncomfortable silence for all concerned.

She looked at me like I was a mental case, and she said yes.

And though I was there at that first meeting in the Skeleton Key, and though I was there when she said yes, what I didn't know was that years after my death I would be there again, watching the edited highlights, out of sight - concealed like some kind of voyeuristic twitcher - and that as I watched myself fall in love with Eliza and watched her agree to become my wife, I would fall in love with her all over again.

CHAPTER ELEVEN

Three Wongs Don't Make A Wight, At Wong's
Wosh And Winse

There's a launderette that sits in the shadow of
the Authority buildings. Nobody goes there, but
vans go in and vans come out and the whole
place throws off a cloud of steam and a stink of
detergent. It's run by the Wongs, three sisters
who lead a secret double life, and the
illuminated sign above the door bears the name
"Wosh And Winse". The triplets are the eyes
and ears of the underground, as they sit
brazenly, right under the sniffing nose of the
Authority.

They may be ladies, but they have some big
brass balls, the size of goose eggs. Sitting in
their cave of damp towels and once-dirty sheets,
their influence radiates out like a web. They are
spoken of in hushed tones all through this place,
and they are the real deal. I've seen plenty of
strange things since I've been here, but the
Wongs... they've been here a long time, and if
anyone has access to the knowledge that will
explain Loupe, it's them.

Of course, nothing's free, and they do like a good trade. Never go to the Wongs and ask for their price without being prepared to haggle - they expect it, they insist on it - it's all a part of their mystique, and their style. They like the game as much as, no, more than the prize - and you'd better talk them down, because they are like the genies of the lamp, their prices have hidden corners and conditions that will take you by surprise. I've bought information from them before, and I've paid dearly for that information, but nonetheless I'm here again - but when the stakes are this high, you've got to be prepared to take a few risks.

I arrived at the launderette to seek an audience with the Wongs, and finagled my way past their burly sumo guards with my usual charm and moxie. They nest at the back of the building, and I tell you what - it's a jungle in here. It's hot and it's humid, the kind of place that makes you think you might catch mildew at any second - these kind of atmospheric conditions will play havoc with my fur, I'll go all curly and frizzy. I wove between the steaming machines and piles of hot clothes, four paws to the floor and making no eye contact with the Wongs' staff - there was always something off about them, something that makes their eyes point in slightly different directions. Something always seemed a bit voodoo around Wong's Wosh And Winse, but I guess that's the kind of thing that helps keep your overheads down. I found myself at the door to their office, and knocked.

"Carmen, lid dull cayenneine friender-vowels!"

Three voices spoke as one from the other side of the door, and I nudged it open and padded inside. The smell was much stronger in here, and the jungle-heat was stifling. The decor was non-existent as such, and nor was their any furniture in the room, but the walls and floor were piled high with damp clothes, in some places still steaming. Where the piles threatened to topple, loops of string and hastily knotted sleeves held the moist stacks together. Even the ceiling was covered in a net, filled with more laundry, which periodically dripped fluid from above. Steam was being piped into the chamber from somewhere, and a haze hung over the place, like some kind of grotesque sauna filled with discarded garments.

The Wongs themselves reclined in the piles, each of them small and wet, nuzzled into the clothing as if trying to disappear into an alternate universe of laundry. They were virtually indistinguishable, short of frame but long of limb, hair dark and lank and hanging in clumps over their faces. Their skin had a strange matt shine, like they'd been smeared in vaseline, and droplets of moisture clung to them like barnacles to a hull. Each of them eased themselves forward with a horrid slurping sound, pockets of steam escaping from behind them as they creaked out of their nests. I don't know where the Wongs are from, originally, they've been around longer than me, which is already longer than I care to remember. They always speak in unison, and in a strange and nonspecific accent - they're hard to understand at the best of times, which at the very least forces you to pay attention. And you really want to pay attention where the Wongs are concerned, or they will snare you up in their laundry bag of tricks before you know what's going on.

"Sew, Misster Jew Jew Poppy. Eaters baner lang toime. Peer hapsis scissor sew shall call?"

"It has, " - a social call indeed, they knew full well that I wouldn't be here unless I needed something, but we have to keep up appearances, right? - "but I'm afraid I'm here on business, not just a friendly chat."

"Ash aim. Wheel awl weighs hover minuet four yew, justice cat chin uptime."

"That's good to know, and I'll make a point of bringing a bottle next time."

"Eggs sealant. Fern how, weasel sticker tubes nizz."

"Thanks, well here's the deal. My current client, Loupe, has started exhibi-"

"Warn fing, beef or yukon tinew. Yews till owe us frommer lass tiem."

"Yeah I know, but I'm good for it."

"Thatch war chews head beef oar."

"I really am this time, you can take my word for it."

"Wheel knee d'amour"

And there it was. I hate this voodoo hoodoo nonsense - the price always comes, well, at a price. It's like doing a crossword with a genie that keeps magicking the clues around the place. What I wanted was to get the hell out of there, to have nothing more to do with this gruesome threesome, but if anyone had the knowledge to tie Loupe down, it was the Wongs. I looked from one to the other and the third. I hated that hungry look they got when they knew a deal was going to go their way, and even though I knew it was a bad idea - three million can buy you a lot of renegotiation tickets, with plenty of change to keep a good dog in clover. I nodded.

"Your fur."

"All of it?"

"Yes. Atwell grobe ack, no?"

"Just the fur, right? You're not planning on skinning me or some freaky thing like that?"

"Juice darfour."

I pause - it's all classic voodoo - a lock of hair, a true name, something personal gives you power over a person. Who knows what hinky trickery they're planning on cooking up with all my lovely winter coat, but I suspect it's simpler than that - I don't think they want to hit me with any weird sorceries, I think they just want to humiliate me because I didn't pay them the last time I came to them for help. A smile splits each of their faces like a fresh wound, and a gleeful light shines in their deep set eyes.

"Tie miss shored, Misster Jew Jew. Anne tie miss monet. Dew knot ways tower time. Deicide."

"Fine. I'm in.", I know I'm going to regret this.

"Thin teal aswad jewel knead foam muss."

I told them the story, about what had happened to Loupe, and how I thought he'd escaped by harnessing his impossible new abilities. I said I needed to catch up with him to help him, but that he might not want to be helped, so I needed some way of coercing him into sticking around. I didn't tell them about the Authority, nor did I mention the money - it's good to keep a bit of knowledge to yourself, gives you wiggle room for renegotiation later when the poop hits the rotating air circulation device.

The Wongs conferred amongst themselves - a high pitched incomprehensible jabber, rising in pitch and intensity. They drew closer to each other, and the room started to feel even more oppressive than it already did, the steam seeming to drift with more purpose, forming a vaporous whirlpool around the three figures, coalescing around them like a galaxy in miniature, then pulling in and enveloping them in an obfuscating cloud that completely hid them from view. A sulphurous odour rose, growing more intense as their babbling reached an ear-splitting crescendo. Finally there was a crack, like a whip driving the steam away. The Wongs stood before me, the central one holding a small blue spotted egg in his open palm.

"Theseus four yew, Missed a Jew Jew. Cracker oh-pen wendelou pissin yore site. Twills low hymn down. Twill bine dim tooth his thyme. Then yukon dew war chew muss."

I took the egg, it had the sulphurous smell on it, subtle but present. The Wongs looked at me eagerly, one pulling a straight razor from a pocket in the nearest wall. Clearly I wasn't going to get to pay for this favour later.

"One thing, before we do this."

"Yesminster?"

"Do you have a nice suit I could borrow? At least a t-shirt. I'd like to retain some scraps of dignity."

They didn't answer, and two of them held me down while the other one went batshit with the razor. I don't know if you've ever seen a hairless dog, but I can tell you it's not a good look. At least they left me a nice moustache. Once they were done, they dismissed me, and I slunk back into the laundry, and stole some clothes, and I learned that if there's a look worse than a hairless dog, it's a hairless dog trying to wear human clothes. Some well placed belts and string and rubber bands helped, though. I stowed the sulphurous egg in one of my new pockets, and left, trying to think of a way to catch up with Loupe so I could put it to use.

INTERLUDE FIVE

The Ongoing Mental Deterioration Of Charlie Stones

Charlie Stones lay in his bed. He was awake again. Each night sleep seemed to elude him for longer, as the voice in his head grew louder, more insistent. He was fourteen years old, and his parents were worried about him. The group therapy sessions didn't seem to be helping either, but no-one really had any idea how bad it had become.

Oh Charlie, you silly boy. Fact is, your household cat seems harmless, but you keep pushing it, keep teasing it and something is going to give. Did you not think about that? It seems like a soft ball of fur but what you forget is that its a soft ball of fur with teeth and claws. So you wind the thing up and you let it go and it bounces off the walls a bit. Hilarious. Until it bounces at you, claws and teeth and rage and all and this time it won't stop. This time it keeps biting, keeps scratching, keeps drawing blood; which seems to only further fuel its fury.

What are you going to do, Charlie? How much claret does that once-loved family pet have to spill before you crack its head open? How much skin does it have to open before you pin it down with your foot and kick it lifeless?

Charlie stared at the ceiling, tried to will the voice away. He thought about Jenni, who'd joined the group a few months ago. Jenni who seemed so free, so full of life. She'd spoken of the darkness that had tried to take her - and he tried to see the voice as something like that. he knew how real it seemed, but he had to try to hold it in check, like that moment when you wake from a nightmare and have to remind yourself that it's not real.

Perhaps you'd be more humane, Charlie. You'd use your ingenuity, grab a handy blanket or jacket. You could bundle good ole Tiddles up and throw him into a room, shut him in. You could leave him there for an hour, let him calm down. I can picture you slamming that door shut, sliding to the floor to catch your breath as your screeching prisoner throws its insignificant mass against the barrier to try to get to you.

It could happen, Charlie.

What happens when you go back later and is mood hasn't changed? What happens when you open the door and that tiny fiend is on you again, three times more ferocious than when you locked him away? You see my point eventually you have to take the necessary steps. You look doubtful. You're still thinking "Mister Boots is only a small animal, claws or no I could control him."

He imagined the voice came from under his pillow, and tried to smother it, pushing down with all of his might - but it stayed with him, whispering into his mind like a devil on his shoulder.

Fair enough, Charlie, lets ramp it up a bit. How about the family dog? A much bigger animal who you've pushed too far. This is a beast who could really hurt you. This is a creature that could knock you down and tear out your throat. Thousands of years of breeding and training and man's best friend is still a wild animal at heart. How much will it take before you hold him down with his foaming jaws snapping at you, all crocodilian, how much does he need to hurt you before you're pushing your thumbs into his windpipe? You will, Charlie, you'll choke the life out of him as his frantic claws shred your forearms.

He squeezed his eyes tight, and tried to visualise her, sat in the group with her unflappable zen calm. He'd once asked her how she kept herself together so well, after all she'd been through, and she told him that it was because she'd been through it, and come out the other side. She said that surviving was the reward - that you won the game by not losing, and the harder the game proved to be, the greater the prize.

Then there's your sister. Your sister, Charlie. You can't shut her in a room, she has opposable thumbs, just like you. She can work the door handle, and she can use tools. She can wait until you're asleep and creep into the kitchen like a burglar. Silently she can open the drawer, and take out that big, sharp knife. She can tiptoe up the stairs. She's stealthy, Charlie - you were playing hide and seek with her just the other week, you know what a slippery customer she is.

You'll be fast asleep, dreaming your peculiar dreams and she'll be stood by your bed with her eyes all black and glittery. She won't even make a noise, just lean forward and push that blade through your neck. She'll stand silent and staring as you thrash about, bleed out and finally expire. What are you going to do about that, Charlie?

No, of course it will never happen. Probably.

Are you sure, though? All I'm saying is that you have to remember that all of these creatures; cat, dog, sister - they're a threat. All I'm saying is that you have to be careful. All I'm saying is that a wise man would think pre-emptively. I'll leave you to think about that for a while, Charlie. Mull it over when you're lying in bed tonight and all these threats are sneaking around the house.

Mister Boots was locked outside that night. This wasn't normally the case, but somehow the latch on the catflap had been popped closed. He'd pushed at it, and realised he wouldn't be able to get in, so he slipped through the window of the shed and slept in there. And that was for the best.

If he hadn't, he would have found Charlie's door ajar, and slipped in there for a sleep instead, and that night Charlie was on the brink. The unfortunate combination of Charlie's condition and Mister Boots proximity would have finally pushed the boy over the edge. Mister Boots would have been the first casualty - his neck twisted until he stopped struggling, and Hennessy the dog would have followed close behind, the second and bloodier victim of Charlie's waking nightmare.

Charlie's parents would have found him stood outside his sister's bedroom door, the knife in his young hand dripping blood onto the carpet. Charlie's dad would have sustained a number of injuries that would scar him for the rest of his life trying to restrain the boy. The only possible option was to institutionalise him, and Charlie would spend the next few years with the voices medicated into silence - a solution from which he would never fully recover.

But that's not what happened, and the conditions that prevailed that night proved to be an apex in Charlie's mental deterioration. The next day, with Jenni shining in his mind, he spoke openly for the first time about the voices, about the unhelpful thoughts and violent urges that plagued him. Mister Boots lived to fight another day.

CHAPTER TWELVE

'Til Death To Us Part… At Least For A While

I've been watching my life with Eliza, and I've come to the conclusion that I was a horrible boyfriend. I was drunk, miserable for no good reason, snappy, snippy, and generally unpleasant. Watching from my vantage point here beyond the grave (woo, spooky) I could see myself for what I was, a borderline schizophrenic plagued by paranoid delusions of being observed. Of course, I was being watched, but only by me, and there's no way I could have known, so I can only put my terrible behaviour down to some kind of physical defect in my brain. I would lose it over the tiniest things and then disappear, sometimes for days at a time, before coming back as if nothing had happened.

Eliza, on the other hand, was almost my diametric opposite. Kind, giving and forgiving. She took my moods and tantrums and vanishings in her stride, and never tried to change me or fix me or unfuck me. All she ever did was accept me for what I was and love me as best she could. As best as anyone could, I think, with my personality being what it was. At least at first.

I didn't see the changes in her back then, because I was too close, and the change was too gradual. I didn't see the damage I was inflicting on her, how I broke her to pieces one emotional bone at a time. How could I? I was too wrapped up in myself, too busy with my own self-absorbed little world, always indulging my incomprehensible fits of rage instead of trying to comprehend them and become better than them. As the wedding approached, as we headed towards the moment when I would tie her inexorably to me, and seal both of our terrible fates, I didn't once notice how she smiled less, how she lost pieces of herself, how I eroded her spirit. I didn't ever see the moment when love became acquiescence, but that moment happened.

I could see it now though, and as our wedding night approached I found myself hating the living me, and found myself constantly wishing I could push through into that reality to give myself the kicking I so rightly deserved - I nearly did it on so many occasions, just like I did with Spigot, but then I remembered what it was like being me. How I saw those monsters hiding around every corner - clearly future-dead me popping up to give myself a good slapping wasn't going to be conducive to a future of quality mental health. Then again - I already knew what my future held, and quality mental health wasn't high on the list of its notable features. Still, I couldn't bring myself to interfere with myself - so I guess some things do change when you're dead.

The big day finally arrived. The old me had spent the night before getting ludicrously wasted and throwing inappropriate amounts of money I didn't have at strippers, and my very forgiving best man was doing his best to pour me into my suit and make me smell a little better than I did. It seemed I was barely conscious. I couldn't believe I'd ever managed to make it to the wedding, let alone actually marry Eliza. Moreover, I couldn't believe that she didn't take one look at me and walk straight out of the door, leaving me to finish my days in my own bitter pickle jar, but when the time came to say "I do", she did.

She was a vision, more immaculate than ever, gliding gracefully up the aisle as I stood there reeking and shambolic. Her family and friends (you couldn't really call them our friends, it was clear what side that bread was buttered on, and rightly so - I was a barely tolerated stain on her friendships) sat as the ceremony unfolded. I'm amazed that no-one stood up at that part where you're supposed to declare reasons why the wedding shouldn't go ahead. I could think of at least a hundred. But no-one said anything, and I could feel the air of despondent resignation in the room as she did the deed and made me her husband. Watching from my vantage point I could see the truth, though, and that smile that I remembered from that day was drawn on like a marker pen face on a balloon, about as genuine as a title deed for the moon. I have no idea why she did it, what sense of duty made her fulfil this obligation.

That night, after the muted reception of fake enthusiasm and invented good wishes, she finally broke. It was in the hotel room, we were due to fly on our honeymoon the next day, and the years of putting up with me finally snapped something inside her. I'd got drunk again at the party, way too drunk. Another day spoiled, the one day that should have been hers out of the hundreds she'd devoted to me. It all spilled out of her at once, the dam holding back my crimes against her collapsing in one catastrophic eruption. Rather than being the grovelling, apologetic ball of contrition I should have been I responded the way I always did - I screamed abuse back at her. The things I said were so terrible, undigestible images dredged up from the worst corners of my unpleasant traitor of a living mind, that I could feel nothing but relief when I watched myself storm out into the night. She sat there, on the bed, still wearing her wedding dress, tears flooding her face.

An hour passed, and the grief consuming her was too much to bear. When you push something, nudge something on a job, it's like interacting with the real world through a clear rubber sheet - it resists your attempts to get at the real world by stretching against you, returning the force you exert on it. But I reached out to it and I pushed, and felt it stretching further and further - to the point that the pressure felt like it might break my fingers, but then something else happened. I felt that fabric tear. I closed my eyes and probed around with my fingers until I found the hole, and then started to work at it, make it wider, until I could push myself through that thin film that separated our two realities. I stood there in the hotel room in numb shock at what I'd done. Eliza was sat on the bed, her back to me, with her head in her hands. I cleared my throat and spoke from the darkened corner of the room where I'd somehow invaded reality from beyond the grave.

"I'm so sorry."

Poor Eliza nearly had a heart attack. I walked around the bed and stood in front of her. I know I was recognisably Luke, but different. Older. Eliza, though, was more than a little tipsy from the party, and I didn't want to deny her the idea that for once, I was doing the right thing. It was the first time in a long time she had heard me apologise and mean it. I poured out all the apologies I should have made back then, each one amplified a hundredfold by years of guilt and grief and shame. I sat down beside her, and held her, and she let me - which reminded me that this was the defining feature of our relationship, I did stuff, and she let me.

While Luke was off getting even more blind drunk than he already was, I was there with Eliza. As Luke was out destroying our newly minted marriage, it was me in that hotel room fixing it with tearful apologies and promises of change. As Luke obliterated any memory of the events of his wedding night, I was making our wedding night happen - and as Luke languished in bar after bar until he was thrown out - Eliza and I conceived our son, and afterwards she slept, and I had to leave, to return to this place that I should never have come from, and in the morning Luke was back, and she assumed that he had been there all along. Some kind of reset button had been activated. Luke awoke with no idea of what had happened the night before, but Eliza was his wife, and soon they would discover that they were going to become a family.

This was the point at which something changed in Luke. The darkness in him somehow dissipated, and he started to turn his life around. The fears, the shadows, all seemed to leach out of him. Whatever pollutant had followed him out of my mother's womb seemed to be flowing away. Each day a little more of it rose off him like a dark mist, but it didn't dissipate. It gathered, it pooled in the house - a storm cloud waiting to reach a critical mass and unleash its power. When it was ready, and the better Luke got, the more it swelled with potential, it started to flow into Eliza, into our unborn son. From where I was stood, you could see the smoke gather around her ever-swelling belly, you could see as it settled onto her skin and was absorbed. Luke became the man he'd always had the potential to be, brighter, interested, attentive - he cared for Eliza, and showed her the love that I'd promised her that night in the hotel room, and Eliza thought that everything had somehow been fixed, that we'd reached some kind of tipping point - but she couldn't see the sinister forces at work, she didn't know about me, about how I was involved. Luke and Eliza started to build the perfect life that she'd seen in him all those years ago, the potential the she'd somehow sensed being realised, unaware that the blight had simply crept away from Luke and burrowed into her like some kind of parasitic worm.

It took me a little while to catch on to what I'd done, but the moment I realised I knew I was in serious trouble. I had to find the Juju Puppy, and fast - though I didn't think anyone would have any idea of what happened when the dead impregnated the living.

CHAPTER THIRTEEN

You Can't Make An Omelette Without Breaking Some Eggs

Fortunately, Loupe found me. I was sat in the bar, trying desperately to think of a way to contact him, and I was drawing blanks all the way. It was all well and good having the egg from the Wongs that would capture him, but you can't capture what's not there. Which is when Loupe walked into the bar and sat down next to me. Sometimes it's like the universe is taking the piss out of you a little bit. Obviously the first thing he noticed was my exciting and fashionable new look. I would need to think fast.

"What's with the weird outfit? And what happened to your face?"

"Your friend Gaunt, that's what. Thanks for just leaving me to his tender mercies. The Authority really aren't a friendly bunch, you know. Besides, this is what the fashionable hound will be wearing in Paris next spring, I'm just ahead of the curve. Fur is so passe, the moustachioed skinhead look is where it's at."

"I'm sorry, Juju. The moustache looks good though."

"Give your apologies to the barman."

Loupe got the drinks in, and I took a moment to get myself together. I could feel the weight of the egg in my pocket, and it was starting to feel heavier by the minute. I kept catching whiffs of its sulphurous odour. I hoped Loupe wouldn't smell it, though I was fairly sure he wouldn't, I have a very sensitive nose. We took to our alcohol, and I got Loupe to bring me up to speed on what happened after he abandoned me on that train. It took some time, and I think we can all agree that his tale was something of an emotional rollercoaster.

"Holy shit, Loupe. I'm pretty sure that you're not supposed to do that."

"I know."

"I mean... the dead creating the living? That can't be right.", I drained the glass, "Give me a minute, I need to go and cock my leg. I'll nip to that lamp-post outside."

I headed outside, and wandered down the street to the nearest payphone, picked up the receiver, then dialled Gaunt's number. I felt like a prick, but gave him the address of the pub, and told him to get his people there as soon as possible. My treachery almost complete, I headed back into the bar. I paused at the lamp-post though - I may be a traitor, but I'm not a liar.

"That's better."

"What do you think happens now?"

"I don't know what's happening to you, Loupe, but it's way outside my experience. I'm trying my best to help you, but I've never heard of anything like this before. Whatever it is that's going on, it seems to me that you're getting stronger, and I don't know what the repercussions of the stuff you're doing are."

"But you think it could be bad?"

"I think it could be catastrophic - look at Gaunt, I'm sure they don't chuck those kind of resources at minor problems - whatever you are, whatever you're becoming, you're clearly a threat to the Authority's plans. I can't imagine they drag off innocent citizens to their dungeons and beat seven bells out of them for unpaid parking tickets."

"Good point. So what do you suggest?"

"Look, I know some people - we can talk to them. They're old school post-mortem, you know what I'm saying? They've got a lot of knowledge, and might just know something that can help. Until we do, perhaps you could lay off playing around with the fabric of time and space for a little while."

"I think it's a bit late for that. What about Eliza?"

"Well she certainly got something stiffer than she was expecting. Seriously though, it can't be good. Do you think it will be a zombie baby or something?"

"I was there already, when he was born, remember? Before I died. There was nothing wrong with him. He was a perfectly healthy, normal baby."

"That was then, this is now. Maybe you've changed things."

"Maybe."

My ears pricked to the sound of tyres outside. They'd arrived. I reached into my pocket, and pulled out the egg. Loupe turned to look at me as I lifted it up, and gave it a solid tap on the edge of the bar - and time stood still for a minute (obviously that's not right, time can't stand still for a period of time, but you'll just have to allow me the logical inconsistency). The shell of the egg splintered, fault lines radiating out from the point of impact like a bad day in Los Angeles in miniature, and the egg started to open up as the fissure circumnavigated its surface, the membrane beneath tearing apart to release its contents.

The cracking sound echoed, and fed back on itself, reverberated around the bar. Then everything started to happen at once. Loupe's hands instinctively cupped his ears to protect them from the noise, and for me it was even worse, damn dog ears - the noise was deafening, and the whole place started to whip up like a hurricane. I squinted against the rising wind, as Loupe fell from his stool and landed awkwardly on the floor in some kind of spasm, his body rigid and his arms stiff at his sides. The egg's contents dripped from the counter to the floor and pooled up around his left foot. The albumen started to creep towards him, moving like mercury, and the yolk glowed with an eerie phosphorescence, like the eye of some Lovecraftian creature. I nearly always break the yolk when I crack an egg, and some distant part of my brain felt a peculiar discordant satisfaction that I kept this one intact.

"What the fuck?", his teeth were gritted, and he was all pulled in against himself, as if he was being tied by an invisible cord looped multiple times around his body. He strained to escape, but he'd never been the most impressive physical specimen, and those hidden cords were clearly too much for him. He stopped struggling, and I saw his eyes cloud as his mind turns inward, trying to pull the same trick he used to escape on the train, but there was no chance - whatever else you might say about the Wongs, they always provide reliable product. It looked as though he was thoroughly (if you'll excuse the pun) egg-bound.

The contents of the egg continued their sluglike journey up his body, curling around his neck like a slimy caress, before enveloping his face. Loupe struggled against it, fighting to avoid being smothered - the egg pushed its way between his lips, invaded his nostrils and ears. Loupe was almost fitting at this point, twitching for breath, his feet dancing the jig of a hanged man as the invisible ropes squeezed his burning lungs and the egg blocked his airways... and then the egg was gone, somewhere into Loupe's body

- preventing him from doing whatever he needs to do to get away.

The doors burst open, a little over-dramatically if you ask me, and in strode Gaunt, with Huey, Dewey and Louie close behind. They'd put on their Sunday best shiny boots and SWAT-style body armour for the occasion, and you could see in their faces that they were loving it. They surrounded Loupe as he struggled on the floor, and Gaunt gives him an experimental toe-prod.

"Nice to see you again, Mister Loupe. Let's see how tricky you can be today, hmm?"

Loupe's ignored Gaunt completely, his gaze fixed on me. He could scarcely believe that I, his grief counsellor, therapist, and best friend would have sold him out. He didn't look angry, even, more bewildered - as if he could never for a moment have conceived that I would ever turn on him. Just goes to show, you can never really know anyone. Through the confusion, he addresses me.

"You prick."

OK, maybe I misread him. Maybe he was a bit angry. As if he was the only one with a right to be pissed off - after all he was the one who left me on that train, who dumped me on the not-so-tender and not-so-merciful mercies of Gaunt and his friends. Hell, what I did was justified, after what he did to me. My motive for selling him out was pure, simple revenge. It was his own fault, so I had the moral high ground. At least I did until Gaunt handed me a briefcase containing the three million payoff. He made sure to take a moment to open it as well, to show me that the money was there - but I think mainly to show Loupe why he was in this situation, and to make it clear that I'd betrayed him. He closed the case, flipped the catches shut, and handed it to me. I took the handle in one shameful paw. It wasn't as heavy as you'd think, at least in terms of physical weight. Loupe was vibrating with rage.

"You sold me down the river for money? Seriously?"

"Mister Loupe, your friend didn't sell you out for money.", Gaunt told him.

"So what's that in the case?"

"He sold you out for a shitload of money."

"I didn't feel good about it, Loupe.", I interjected - I hate it when I get whiney.

"Can't say I'm in the mood for dancing myself, Juju. I hope it buys you everything you want.", he spat.

I stood there looking wretched, holding my briefcase of money. Dewey clearly felt a moment of compassion for my plight, and took the opportunity to give Loupe a hard boot in the stomach. Loupe doubled up with the impact, so Huey helped him to straighten up again by applying a well placed kick to the small of his back. I heard something crack, and hoped it wasn't Loupe's spine.

All three of Gaunt's goons started to take turns, like a horribly violent game of pass the parcel where no-one is in charge of stopping the music. As Loupe was beaten into unconsciousness he didn't take his eyes off me for a moment, staring me down between each hefty kick and clout. Finally his eyes misted over and he passed out. Huey, Dewey and Louie picked him up and dragged him off to their van. I stood and watched them go, my stomach sick with shame.

"So what happens now?"

"You go about your business, Mister Juju. Enjoy your money, you've earned it."

"I mean what happens to Loupe?"

"You're suddenly concerned for his welfare?"

"Of course I -"

"Aren't you just a mass of contradictions."

"So what are you going to do?"

"What do you think we're going to do? We're going to find out what we can from him, then we're going to kill him, and cut him into little pieces, and see what we can find out from the little pieces. All very scientific. He's clearly a valuable specimen, so we'll do our best to not lose any of the bits."

He turned and strode out of the door, and I heard the van door slam, the engine start, and Loupe being driven away to his terrible fate. I stood there like a shaved dog should, like a bad dog should, holding onto my briefcase. I'd like to tell you that the three million didn't help take some of the edge of that guilt, but really it did. I walked over to the bar and ordered a drink, then took myself off to a booth to drown my sorrows.

Some time later, my sorrows had proved to be pretty tenacious swimmers, and were even now managing to tread water. I, on the other hand, was sinking fast - which was when I felt the blistering pain in my head, as if a boiling hot needle was being pushed through my pickled brain. Then a voice I recognised spoke - you know how your voice sounds when you plug up your ears so you only hear yourself inside your head? Like that.

{{{Meat stir Jew Jew, wean id chew tock. NOW. Weirs ending sum won chew peak yew hop.}}}

Looks like the Wongs found more use for my fur than just making me look silly. God damn voodoo. I saw the headlights of a car pulling up outside. I sighed a heavy sigh, and dragged my sorry arse out of the door.

INTERLUDE SIX

A Night On The Tiles With A Cat Named Mister Boots

Mister Boots was something of a legend in the area. In the society of cats that inhabited the local streets, he classified as "kind of a big deal". Sure, he didn't look like much, but appearances could be deceptive. The thing was that a lot of these cats were well looked after, well fed, and a little too comfortable. Not to say that Mister Boots wasn't, but some instinct in him told him to stay frosty. He might be a pet, but he also fought and fucked harder than any other kitty on the block, which made him top dog in cat terms.

In part, it was the boy - he could smell something off about that boy. Mister Boots had a finely tuned sense of peril, and Charlie exuded danger like a tramp smells of booze. So he kept himself alert, and kept himself in shape, ready to run or fight as the situation demanded. Of course, this meant walking a fine tightrope - the humans fed him, so he had to play the loveable pet as well. Mister Boots lived his whole life this way, pretending to be what he wasn't. A few minutes spent asleep on a comfortable lap would make sure the food bowl kept being filled, and then he could always supplement his diet when he did his rounds. There was no shortage of snacks around for a cold-hearted, trained killer such as Mister Boots.

The other cats around his patch, well - all the queens wanted him, and all the toms wanted to be him. He got what he wanted, when he wanted - and woe betide any cat who tried to get in his way. Most of them backed down at a suitable display of hissing and spitting, and those that didn't found themselves on the wrong end of his well honed propensity for immediate and brutal violence. Usually that was a lesson they only had to learn once, and for the most part it didn't even come to that, most of the toms round these parts didn't have the balls to take on Mister Boots. Literally.

Tonight though, he caught the smell of a new tomcat on the block. His fur rose instinctively, as he sniffed the scent the interloper had left. Not only that, but right by his own back gate - and this wasn't the weak piss left by the saggy, soft, neutered locals. This was a proper tom, he could smell the battle in his marking. He glanced around. The street was quiet, but this piss was fresh enough to tell him the newcomer couldn't be too far away, probably trying to fuck his women. Well, he'd picked the wrong patch to try to make his own, and no mistake. Mister Boots leapt onto the wall, and started to stalk the intruder.

He found him a couple of streets away, balls-deep in a yowling queen - a demure little tabby from his inner harem. Protocol insisted that Mister Boots wait until they could disengage, but he made sure the visitor knew he was there and ready to fight, flexing his claws and screaming a challenge from the rooftop opposite. The new cat looked up at him, without a pause in his humping, and hissed. The tabby tried to break away, but was grabbed on the neck by a vicious bite.

Mister Boots took the opportunity to study the interloper, and decided to name him Big Grey Bastard, and big he definitely was - bigger than Mister Boots by a fair margin. His fur wasn't well kept, a matted grey mass that clung to his body sporadically, and he wore the scars of a lot of fights. Boots weighed him up - he was a large opponent, sure, and clearly strong, but those scars indicated a lot of fights that hadn't gone his way. The simple fact that he was wandering into another territory suggested that he was perhaps not well balanced in a brawn to brains ratio.

Big Grey Bastard finished his business, and the tabby slunk away down the wall and into the night. Mister Boots would have to re-establish his superiority with her later, but first it was time to get his fight on. He leapt nimbly across to where Big Grey Bastard stood awaiting his challenge. He could sense that the new tom expected him to be cowed, to start proceedings with a bit of display, puffing himself up and making noise to try to drive him away. He was an experienced fighter, though, and knew this would be pointless - so he took advantage of the expectation and pushed the element of surprise, pouncing straight onto Big Grey Bastard with all claws blazing. He drew first blood from his enemy's muzzle, and they both tumbled into the alley below.

This was not the play fighting of weaning kittens - this was full on street fighting, hard, dirty, and deadly serious. Blood and fur flew as the two opponents each tried to gain advantage over the other. He tried to take advantage of his speed and stay to each side, get behind the grey giant - the couple of times blows managed to land he was almost knocked senseless by the raw ferocious strength of his challenger. Mister

Boots, though, was like a master swordsman facing off against a lumbering wrestler, and soon Big Grey Bastard could see he was defeated, and took the only option available to him - he turned tail and ran.

Normally, that would be it, but tonight Mister Boots felt a cold rage in him and took off in pursuit - there was no way he was going to allow this one to come back and try again. Like a pair of insane frenchmen on a parkour racetrack they sprinted like felines possessed, but Big Grey Bastard had a greater reserve of stamina than the smaller cat, and made his escape.

Mister Boots looked around, and realised to his horror that he had no idea where he was. It was late, it was dark, and he was lost. He looked around at the darkened houses, and tried to figure out what to do next. They say cats can see things other people can't, that they can look into the world beyond this one. If so, that explains why Mister Boots stopped and looked at an invisible figure in front of him, his ears pricked as if listening for instructions, before heading purposefully towards one of the nearby houses.

CHAPTER FOURTEEN

Things Take A Wong Turn

The car was spacious and comfortable, and unfortunately driven by one of the Wongs' boggle-eyed employees, who had a fairly haphazard approach to cornering. That, combined with the suspension of an industrial grade bouncy castle and an in-car heating system that apparently worked by opening an interdimensional portal to the heart of the sun, did not a happy puppy make. If you bear in mind the amount of drinks I'd put away after Gaunt and his cronies had dragged Loupe's unconscious form away, you could hardly blame me for the state of the upholstery by the time we'd arrived at our destination, Wong's Wosh And Winse. The car stopped, and I pushed the door open, letting the foul smell of my involuntary emissions out. I retched again, and took a deep breath or three, the cool air helped to settle my roiling stomach. I tried to prepare myself for the Wongs, for the chemical sauna that lay within, tendrils of foul smelling vapour waving to me from the open door.

I entered their damp nest, trying to keep my head high. As ever, it was jungle humid in there, making each breath a laboured drink for my straining lungs. The Wongs were settled in to their piles, each one's hands moving around the laundry stacks around them, caressing the wool blends, the polyesters, and fingering the cottons idly.

"Sew gladiator hear, Jew Jew. Weir sume ower liddle ch-arm diddits werk? Yorf rend has-been apres hen did?"

"Yeah, it's done. Don't suppose I can have my fur back, can I?"

"Know. Yore fore is too yews full, as yews awe."

"You know they have telephones now, right?"

"Weir awled fash earned."

"Clearly."

"Wee brow toe yew hear, bee course sump apple wont chew sea yew."

"Oh so it's a party? If I'd known in advance, I'd have worn a nicer frock."

You know, it's not easy to maintain my brand of John McClane wisecracking facade in the face of adversity - there are very few people who can pull it off, and when circumstances turn against you, it takes an absolute force of will to maintain the illusion of being a carefree wit-about-town. So when the door behind me opened and The Mouse stepped into the room flanked by a couple of heavies, and Pilter skulking around in the background, it was my big opportunity to prove how incredibly cool I was with some flippant action hero style line. Unfortunately, Bruce Willis I am not, so I completely flubbed it.

"Oh shit."

"Oh shit indeed, son."

"How you doin' Mouse? You were next on my list to come and visit - I got your money."

"It's been a long time, seems you've been avoiding me. Pilter here says he bumped into you recently. I assumed you'd skipped town, so imagine my surprise when I learned you were still around, rubbing my face in your debt."

The Mouse is, by any measure, a big lad. Naturally, that's why they call him The Mouse -

it's one of those Little John kind of deals, ironic in that ten thousand spoons when all you need is a knife way that only Alanis Morissette could truly understand. He was what you might describe as a man of business. He wore suits with a fetching pinstripe, and if you were in a jam, in need of some emergency funds for whatever project was making your fur itch, he was the man to go to. He wasn't even a particularly unfair practitioner of the moneylending arts - but his methods concerning those who failed to pay up and those who tried to muscle in on his territory were notorious.

He'd found a niche here, and intended to milk it for all it was worth, suckling at the udder of the underworld's underbelly. Unfortunately for me, I was one of those people who'd crossed him. Something told me it wasn't just knuckles the two shaven headed bouncer types he'd brought with him were here to crack. I resigned myself to that fate, but I really wished that fleabag Pilter wasn't there to enjoy it after I'd got one over on him. There's nothing more annoying than an irritating weasel enjoying revenge by muscular proxy.

"Tell you what, how about I pay you double?", that would take a sizeable chunk out of my bankroll, but it's hard to spend your reward money on ale and whores when your skull has a dent in it. Pilter snorted, as if he had any say in the matter. "Shut it, Pilter," I growled, "The grown ups are talking." The Mouse gave him a quick glance, and he dipped his head and backed up.

"Well, Juju - I'm going to agree to that, and you can certainly pay me. But that's not why I'm here right now. I'm here representing a collective of what you might call... vested interests. A certain party has apprised us of various circumstances which have caused my associates and myself some concern."

"You're talking about Loupe? Well he's not going to be a problem any more. I took care of it."

"No, we're not talking about Loupe. In fact, Loupe is the one who told us."

"That can't be right - The Authority has Loupe, and they're going to..."

"Kill me?"

I kept looking forward, at The Mouse and the Wongs, feeling the creeping horror of someone who's just said a bad thing about someone after hanging up a phone, then spotted that the receiver isn't quite back on the hook properly.

"He's behind me, isn't he?"

I turned, and there he was, as large as life. He wasn't looking great, I can tell you - one side of his face was covered in one giant purple bruise, his eye swollen and barely open more than a slit. His left arm was held in a makeshift sling, and his shoulder looked strangely out of alignment. His clothes were torn and bloody and all in all he looked like an extra from a zombie movie with an excellent make-up budget. He regarded me with his good eye, and I looked at the floor.

"Don't worry, Juju - I've already forgiven you, on account of what you're going to do. You're going to save me, with the help of these good gentlemen", he gestured at The Mouse and the Wongs.

"I don't understand."

"Right, it's actually pretty simple. Right now, I'm shackled in one of the sublevels of the Authority building, while Gaunt is trying to decide which bit of me to cut off first...", and he outlined what was going on.

This Loupe was not the Loupe I'd sent to his death. Well, it was, but this was him after I'd gone on to rescue him from Gaunt's clutches. I pointed out that I honestly had no plans to go and rescue him, but apparently that didn't matter. Here's how he explained it - the Loupe who was talking to me, the future Loupe, came back to now to arrange this meeting. He knew to arrange this meeting because I told him to arrange the meeting when I rescued him. So, I do this because he told me to do it because I told him to do it because he told me to do it... you get the idea. I wasn't shy about expressing how little sense that made, but you couldn't avoid the inescapable logic of it. I realised that at this point I was stuck in an inevitable path. I had no choice, I was going to have to rescue Loupe. The Wongs chimed in.

"Off coors, yew most dress queue Loupe."

"It's true, Juju - there is no choice, because the world needs me right now."

"What are you a superhero or something? 'The world needs me' - you're not Batman."

"I'm something like that though."

He explained to me that after we'd made the daring escape from the Authority that we hadn't done yet, he'd come to see the Wongs about the problem of his creation of a baby from beyond the grave. This turned out to be quite a big deal - the Wongs knew of occasions where it had happened before, and confirmed that these situations had never turned out well, coinciding with the beginnings of the darkest periods in human history. Look, I'm not saying that Adolf Hitler was definitely some kind of beyond-the-grave horror baby... but that's pretty much the long and the short of how it works, and he's a good go-to example when you want to demonstrate a really bad person who makes the world measurably worse.

Anyway, the problem is that someone needs to deal with that baby, and to make sure of everything we need someone who can get to the source of the problem, and get into the real world to sort it out. The Wongs said it was a question of balance, that Loupe's abilities were born of the universe trying to counteract the presence of such a disturbing force in its fabric.

"So you've implanted the antichrist in your newlywed wife from the future beyond, and now you're the brand new Jesus, here to save the day? Is that what you're telling me? Delusions of grandeur much?"

Of course, I realised later on that I'd been duped. Utterly and completely had. But right now, I was in this up to my neck. The Mouse was sending the two blockmen to help me get into the building and find Loupe - apparently Loupe was paying him handsomely for providing the muscle for the extraction. The Wongs were here to provide the means to actually release him from the magic of the egg. They got up from their perches and together pulled aside some wet sheets to reveal a gilded cage, containing a chicken. A fucking chicken. It fixed me with a beady eye. This is what happens when you deal with people like this - you end up in a weird staring match with a chicken.

"What's that going to do? Vacuum the egg back into it's arse?"

"Yew muss sack reef ice hymn when yew fined Loupe. Hit well comp elite tea sigh cull. Thee chick hen and thee egg. The egg hand the chick hen."

"It's a messy job, Juju - you told me to tell you to bring an apron. But you also told me that you forgot the apron I told you to bring, so I'm afraid your nice suit is going to get ruined."

I shouldn't have been too surprised that it was a chicken, really. I've said it before and I'll say it again. God damn voodoo. In the end I picked up the chicken and just accepted that I was on an inevitable path - clearly I was going to do this, I was going to rescue Loupe - if I wasn't then Loupe couldn't be here telling me I was going to do it. The whole mess of it was starting to make my head hurt.

Then Loupe pulled me aside and told me the rest of the plan, and we got me kitted out with everything I needed, and he promised to look after my briefcase for when I returned.

CHAPTER FIFTEEN

Just Another Day In Gauntanamo Bay

Time had ceased to have any meaning for
Loupe, and not just due to the fact that he'd
developed the ability to move around in it. He
had no idea how long he'd been stood like this,
naked, his arms tied above his head with just
enough play to allow him to reach the floor.
Despite the claims of salt-of-the-earth hard
working types everywhere - there is only so
much standing the human (or post-human) can
take.

The East German Stazi would make their
victims stand for twenty four hours or more -
and this could produce excruciating pain. Over
long periods heart rates would soar, vital organs
would shut down. It didn't take very long for
Loupe to become delusional, detached from
reality. Whenever Gaunt and his glamorous
assistants were out of the room, hidden speakers
bombarded him with a constant and
cacophonous barrage of screaming rock music.
He was fairly sure he hadn't been in this place
for more than a day though. Maybe five. Or

perhaps it had been a few years. Sometimes, the beatings and the questioning felt like a relief.

It didn't seem entirely beyond the realms of possibility that he didn't exist at all, and sometimes he drew some small comfort from the idea that he had nothing to worry about, that he was just a fiction - after all, when you thought about it, the whole situation was utterly ludicrous - a dead man being tortured by a giant bureaucratic organisation in the afterlife, because he's learned to travel in time and... no the whole thing was quite nonsensical, somebody must have just made it up.

Gaunt had a lot of questions, and Loupe had figured that to avoid any excess electrocution of his genitalia, he would try to answer as honestly as he could, telling the whole story. Gaunt had seemed satisfied with the telling of the tale, but was apparently not finished with Loupe by a long chalk. Suddenly, the blistering repeat rendition of Deicide's timeless soft rock ballad "Fuck Your God" stopped, and the door rattled open.

"You know, this is entirely unnecessary.", Loupe's ears still hadn't adjusted to the sudden silence, and the voice sounded like it was coming out of a can. He tried to lift his head, but his entire body was suffused with pain. "Let him down, and bring the poor fellow a chair. I don't know what's wrong with you, Gaunt, we are not common beasts, and in future you should consider treating our guests with a little kindness. The carrot can achieve so much more than the stick, and yet the stick seems to be your default setting."

Loupe kept his eyes shut, hearing footsteps shuffle into the room, and the squeaking of wheels. Hands gripped and supported him as the shackles were removed from his wrists. Bolts of pain burst through his ankles and up his legs as he was lowered to a standing position, and his knees immediately buckled. The hands holding him took the strain, keeping him upright as his legs flopped around beneath him - and was dragged to a chair, and lowered into a sitting position. It was all he could do to keep himself from falling over sideways.

"Now, let's take him somewhere a little more comfortable, and we can have a proper chat."

The chair, Loupe realised, was a wheelchair, and he was pushed out of the room, followed by the new arrival and his entourage. The fluorescent lights in the corridor were terribly bright, and his eyes watered, reducing all visibility of the hospital-like corridors, painted a disturbing shade of institutional beige to a vague blur. It made his head hurt to try to interpret the visual spectrum, so he put his head down again and closed his eyes, passing out for a short while.

When he awoke, he was in an office, an opulent den with plush red carpeting, walls lined with floor to ceiling bookcases, and an enormous carved desk. The room was gently lit with green glass shades, and his eyes started to adjust to the dimmer, friendlier light. The office was warm, a fire lit in the fireplace. He raised his head. To his left, Gaunt was stood to attention, his hands folded behind his back, his expression dark and inscrutable. To his left was a small table, upon which stood a plastic beaker filled with what looked like water. Loupe lifted his arm weakly and reached for it, and although there was many a slip betwixt cup and lip, he succeeded in getting at least some of the water into his mouth, and from there guzzled greedily.

"That must feel a lot better. I'm Nathaniel, by the way."

For the first time, Loupe looked up at the figure behind the desk. He was a large man, clearly muscular beneath his white linen suit. His fairly blocky head was bereft of any hair, and he sat in a large burnished leather armchair. His skin was pale to the point of luminescence, so much so you could almost see the blood moving through his veins. His eyes were pink, like those of an albino rat, without iris or pupil.

Most notable, however, were the pair of giant feathered wings gathered in at his shoulders. The figure stood, and walked around the desk, and the wings trailed behind him, brushing the carpet as they did. Each individual feather was glossy and snow-white, in fact most everything about him was immaculate. As he reached Loupe, he reached out and put a hand on his shoulder - and immediately a feeling of well-being coursed through him, like a tonic racing around his nervous system. Loupe gasped involuntarily, immediately sitting up straighter in his chair.

"What are you?"

The man laughed, "I could ask you the same question. But there'll be time for all that later. First of all, please allow me to extend my deepest apologies for your treatment at the hands of Gaunt. Although he was, strictly speaking, only doing his job - it can be difficult to keep track of what happens at all levels of an organisation this size. You can, although it may be small comfort, rest assured that this will not be permitted to happen again. The truth is, that while Mister Gaunt is a valued resource, representing the arm of the Authority with admirable efficiency, he can sometimes be a little overzealous in his methods. I asked Gaunt to remain here because I want you to understand that I do not condone his actions in this case, and so you can see as I formally reprimand him for his behaviour. You are dismissed, Gaunt."

Gaunt turned stiffly, and left the room, his face impassive - except for a moment as his eyes met Loupe's, and an unspoken message passed between them with the burning intensity of a white hot star. Loupe could see that, whatever his superior might have to say on the subject, their business was by no means finished. "Now, let us get down to business, shall we?", the man clapped his hands together and strode back to his seat, getting comfortable and steepling his fingers before him. He smiled, and Loupe caught a hint of something predatory behind the friendly exterior, a ruthless undercurrent that bubbled through his otherwise affable aura like the momentary expressions on the face of a salesman as he tries to make you think he's on your side.

"You present quite a challenge to us here, Loupe. Yes, quite the challenge. However, I've always been a firm believer that every challenge also brings with it opportunity. Now, you have done some terrible things, though some would quite reasonably argue that you are a product of your environment. As for what has occurred with your wife - well it seems that that all worked out alright in the end, the child is dead, after all, so balance is restored. I know that it hurts, Loupe, but the fact is that the dead simply must never create the living in such a way, and you should take comfort from the fact that a terrible disaster was averted. Well, will be averted. Mister Gaunt will be taking care of the problem for us. I'm truly sorry, because I understand the grief that this causes you. I feel your pain, Loupe, but I hope you understand the necessity of what must be done."

And then Loupe understood - Gaunt was the invisible monster, the creature who had broken his son's bones, who had ended his son's life, and by extension ended his life - and as he remembered the look that Gaunt had given him as he left, he knew that not only was he going to murder his son, and by extension murder him at one remove - Gaunt was going to enjoy it, take pleasure in the atrocities that he would commit, that had ruined everything for Loupe.

"Oh, I'm sorry, did you think you were the only person capable of doing what you do? We have ways and means, though unfortunately they are rather... costly. Which is why I choose to view you, Loupe, as an opportunity. We would love to work with you, Loupe. I know this may seem insane right now, that you may think there is no way you could possibly come to our side, but you'd be amazed how much you can heal given time - and time is something we aren't short of here.

"And believe me, Loupe, working for us is not without it's advantages. You'll find that when you turn your hand to the will of the Authority this place can be very accommodating. We're doing good work, you know. We're maintaining order where otherwise there would be chaos - we're helping the living maximise their potential through the elimination of free will. Well, elimination is a string word. Through the reduction of free will to levels within acceptable parameters.

"What we do is vital to the orderly running of the universe. If you could see it, if you could see those strands of destiny that tie humans together, in their raw state, before we intervene, you'd be horrified - pure chaos, Loupe. Those beautiful lines of light just bending every which way, people making all sorts of decisions and going in any direction they feel like. No, it's an affront to all that makes the world good. If you could see it now, though, if you could see the beauty of all those lines in order, infinite parallel lines of light. Order, the knotted entropic fabric of the universe tamed by the application of mind and will. It is a humbling sight."

Loupe watched as the man drew himself up to his full height, bursting with pride and his wings barely restrained from stretching wide in celebration as the glory of the Authority's mission.

"So let me get this straight, you want me to say thanks for killing my son, and then come and help you destroy people's free will to satisfy some obsessive compulsive urge to make human destiny line up in neat rows and columns on your universal spreadsheet? No offence, but I think you can go and choke on a cock."

Nathaniel's composure flickered, only for a fraction of a second, but long enough for Loupe to see what lay beneath the friendly exterior. He may have been playing the good cop, but when the mask slipped it confirmed Loupe's suspicions that even a good cop round here was a bad cop harbouring a temporary attitude adjustment. That flicker passed on, though, as quickly as it came, and Nathaniel returned to the glowing demeanour of before, but now it seemed like that of a nursery school teacher trying to explain to a small child why he shouldn't bite the other children, and Loupe suspected that Nathaniel might want to bite him instead.

"I understand, Loupe. You're angry. You have every right to be, you've been dealt a shitty hand - and if there was any other option, I'd do this differently - but sometimes you've got to play the cards as they fall. Now, I'm afraid I'm going to have to send you back to your room for a while. Hopefully with a bit of time to reflect you'll start to see things my way."

Nathaniel pushed a buzzer on his desk, and Loupe's captors and torturers swept into the room and wheeled him away through the labyrinthine corridors of the Authority headquarters, and back to his cell. They opened the door, and shoved him inside, the wheels squeaking as he free wheeled across the room until his toes stubbed against the far wall. The door was slammed behind him, the bolts were drawn, and he was plunged into darkness and blessed silence. Loupe closed his eyes, and waited.

INTERLUDE SEVEN

The Fictional Lies Of Alex Jones

Alex Jones knew that if he ever had children, his tendency to enjoy telling lies would cause him to make it my life's work to mislead and deceive them. He would go down in history as the man who produced the most fucked up kids the world ever saw.

He would tell them that mummy is a killbot with a death circuit activated by the tears of children. They will learn that if they want to cry, they must always cry alone. Her arms, he would say, transform into scythes for chopping off childrens' legs and fingers, and that that's why the garden is so well fertilised - with human blood.

He would tell them that father christmas is a grey, wet man with nails for teeth and eyes like gimlets, who crawls down the chimney on sticky fingers like his limbs are broken, and who leaves presents but takes teeth in payment from one child in five with his tiny christmas hammer - and then skitters away leaving traces of smeared, wet soot and a lingering odour of damp and gum disease.

He would teach them the alphabet in the wrong order, and when their teacher tried to correct the damage he had done, he would tell them that their teacher is a murderer. He would say that she knows that children are ripe for harvesting when they do the alphabet her way, and then she wraps them up in carrier bags and leaves them in her crawlspace to die of thirst.

He would tell them that stepping on cracks in the pavement gives them cancer, that chewing pencils causes their skin to become scaly and weep grease, and that eating vegetables will make their eyes swivel so they can only see their brain. He would tell them that all other children are controlled by brain parasites put in their ears by their parents under government instruction, and that he's not going to put one in them but if the government finds out they will send people to cut them open without anaesthetic and see what makes them tick.

He would tell them that cats carry a flesh-eating plague that will make their noses fall off, before slowly demolishing their faces and spiralling them into dementia as it feasts on their brains. That cats try to spread this disease because they are the natural enemy of the human race, and that people who keep cats are their zombie slaves.

He would tell them that there is a race of cannibal creatures at large in the world, who love to feast on the bones of sleeping young. The cannibals sneak into bedrooms during the day and hide in mattresses, waiting for a child to fall asleep, then tear their way out to snatch with their bony, clawed fingers and sink their snaggled, uneven teeth into soft, yielding child-flesh. He would tell them that the only way to be sure they won't fall prey to the cannibals is to stay awake as long as they can.

Alex kept a book, the latest in a series, in which he kept a record of all these ideas, all the lies he could think of to tell the children he would never have. Alex kept away from people as much as possible. He was quite convinced that his strange peccadilloes made him unfit for human consumption, so he locked himself in his house, and he ordered all the things he needed from the internet. Each night, he would pull out his current journal, and write his list of lies as they occurred to him, in his tiny, cluttered handwriting.

That particular night, he'd been standing at his back door, smoking a cigarette, when a fork fell in the sink behind him with a clatter. He turned, startled, and didn't notice as a stray cat by the name of Mister Boots slipped into his house.

He would find the cat later, curled up under his bed, and the discovery wouldn't change his life - Alex didn't have a life. But the arrival of Mister Boots caused just enough disruption. He took a short walk to the local shop, his head down, and even managed to mumble a thank you to the girl at the checkout as he bought some cat food.

The cat stayed with Alex for a few weeks before he moved on, and for the course of those few weeks, he didn't write in his journal, not even once. The day Mister Boots went on his way, Alex searched the streets around his house for hours, and then returned to his old existence. He didn't even realise that he'd missed his annual dental checkup.

CHAPTER SIXTEEN

A Chicken Is Only An Egg's Way Of Making Another Egg

The Authority building was a glorious example of the power of architecture. Many stories high, its brutalist frame hulked into the skyline, a perfect example of how human ingenuity can express every aspect of human nature - in this case the aspect that wants nothing more than to crush the hopes and aspirations of all other humans. A grey and stained cuboid, still standing though riddled with concrete cancer - AHQ was a horrible zombie of a building, loveless and lifeless. If ever a construction was designed to make its inhabitants feel (and by extension behave like) drones in a hive, this was the apex of that dream.

Juju and The Mouse's men slipped into the line entering the building, each of them wearing the false credentials supplied by the Wongs. It wasn't one hundred percent certain how effective the passes were going to be, and the Wongs would only describe them as "probably fine". They waited in line to pass through the security checkpoint. Metre by metre they shuffled forward, until they arrived at the doors, where two security guards awaited them. Juju held up his pass for inspection, and the guard peered at it. "Wait here a moment."

The guard turned and beckoned his fellow over, handing him the passcard. Guard two held it up to the light, turning it for closer examination, then he stepped over to the security terminal and picked up the phone. Juju nervously looked at his companions, who had their hands in their pockets nonchalantly - but that relaxed state was, Juju knew, an illusion - in their pockets they were preparing to strike if necessary, each seemingly careless hand gripping a knife, a gun.

The guard put the phone down, and turned back to Juju, handing him his pass. "That's fine, sir, sorry for the delay." Juju did his best to stifle the sigh of relief, and tried to walk into the building as if he was supposed to be there. Places like this always made him ill at ease - he considered himself to be more of a free-thinking maverick type, and the atmosphere in such monolithic cathedrals of conformity disagreed with him on a molecular level.

He tried to imagine what it would be like doing this every day, join the line, follow the herd, punch in and punch out, and shuddered. In that moment, he developed a greater understand of the melancholy that plagued Loupe - he saw the same maverick tendencies in him, but Loupe lacked the entrepreneurial spirit to evade this aspect of afterlife. No wonder he was miserable.

The trick to infiltrating any building is to act like you belong there. Never skulk, never look around nervously. Keep your head high and move like you have a purpose - and that's exactly what they did. They stepped lively, picked a door and headed for it as if they knew exactly where they were going. In a building this size, it would be a small matter to find an unoccupied room from which to plan their next move. They timed their approach to the door just as a couple of bureaucrats piled high with binders swiped their passcards - kindly they held the door for them, and the grateful overloaded office drones didn't think anything of it as they slipped through the door after them.

Corridor led to corridor, and they kept moving - the plan was to head down, since if you're going to keep a prisoner the most popular option has always been in the dungeon, or as it's now more commonly known, the sub-basement. The Authority didn't go for the old school approach, keeping their unwilling guests in the the top room of the highest tower in the land, since

AHQ didn't have any towers their policy was to go with the bowels of the building. Each time they encountered a stairwell heading down, they took it as far as they could, and discovered that the building had what could only be described as hidden depths.

As they descended, they found they encountered less and less people, which would start to become a problem soon, it's easy to blend into a crowd, to look like you belong in a populated area. Soon they were going to become more noticeable, and someone was bound to ask questions. At that point, this operation was likely to become considerably wetter - but that's what the big guys were for. At this point, Juju was starting to regret not moving into some other line of work - Navy SEAL, for example, even a guy who designs violent video games would have a more appropriate skill set for this kind of situation.

The deepest depths of the building carried a lot more of it's innards on the walls and ceiling, as such parts of a building tend to do - where nobody goes, you don't care so much if your guts are visible, and so electrical conduit and steam pipes ran along the wall. The corridors all started to look the same, and rooms just contained stacks of chairs, boxes of old files, the detritus that builds up around any large organisation over time.

"I'm pretty sure this is the right level. How far down are we? Loupe said sublevel seven. I think we should be ready to... deal with people."

The heavies nodded agreement, and pulled out their weapons. Guns in the right, knife in the left. Somewhere on this level was the room where Loupe was being held, and the plan from this point was a more vigorous brand of infiltration. They crept down the corridors, and eventually found what they were looking for - a low tunnel, fluorescent lit, and at the far end stood two guards. Of course, being guards seven stories underground for a single prisoner for hours at a time is not the kind of task that promotes incredible vigilance, and they didn't even have a chance to go for their guns.

The bodies were swiftly dragged out of the way of the door, and Juju threw the bolts, and pushed the door open. There, sat in a wheelchair, was Loupe. He regarded Juju and the heavies. "Amazing what you can do if you put your mind to it. Don't think for a second I don't still think you're a prick, though.". Juju kept his head down, and pulled an envelope out of his pocket.

"This is for you."

"What is it? Your Christmas list? I wasn't planning on getting you anything, you've been a bad dog."

"Not even a biscuit?"

"Well, maybe a biscuit."

"Thanks. The letter's from you, by the way. You know, future you, it's instructions telling you what you have to do after we get you out of here."

"Juju."

"Yeah?"

"Thanks, man. I know it's all your fault, kind of, but you came through in the end."

Loupe opened the letter, and started to read. When he was finished, Juju opened up the bag strapped to his back. The chicken squawked its indignation at the undignified treatment it had received so far. Gripping it by the neck, he walked over to where Loupe sat, eyebrows raised.

"A chicken?"

"Apparently so - guess there are more things in heaven and earth and all that."

"Do I have to kiss it? Will it turn into a prince and ride us out of here on a white horse?"

"That's frogs."

"Of course it is."

Juju gestured to one of The Mouse's men, who tossed his knife over. Juju tried to catch it, but missed, and it clattered to the floor. Sighing, he picked it up.

"Seriously? Do you like running with scissors too? Someone could lose an eye."

And then he grabbed the chicken by the head, and swung at it's neck with the heavy hunting knife. It took a couple of swipes to get it clean off. The chicken fell to the ground, where its head-free body remained pretty confused about its current status, and proceeded to run all around the place spouting blood willy-nilly. Juju handed the head to Loupe.

"You have to crush the skull in your hand."

Loupe took the chicken's head in his hand and squeezed it, hard. He could feel the thin plates of its skull fracturing, and the wetness inside oozed through his fingers. Immediately, he started to feel lighter - strength returning to him. Power coursed through him as the curse of the egg was lifted. His eyes brightened, and he stood up. He seemed to look through Juju, as if peering into another reality, a thousand yard stare.

"Now that is just the ticket."

And then Loupe vanished, and as the chicken's body gave up the ghost and collapsed in a heap, Juju heard the clatter of boots in the corridor. It sounded like a lot of boots. He reached into his bag and pulled out the other envelope, the one marked "Read this once Loupe is safe", as Boris and Karloff flanked the door, pistols at the ready.

CHAPTER SEVENTEEN

Guns For Show, Knives For A Pro

Oh, what? So I left Juju behind - have you forgotten that he sold me out to Gaunt? What goes around comes around. And besides, I needed that three million to pay The Mouse for his men - it isn't cheap to send a pair of well trained killers on a one-way trip to the bottom of the bay. I do feel bad for them - even henchmen have lives outside being in criminal gangs and beating people silly for a living. Maybe they had interesting hobbies, baking cakes or mending watches. I'll never know - but needs must, and it's pretty clear that when your career choice is "armed henchman", there's a certain degree of inherent risk. If you want to live to a ripe old age and die in your bed surrounded by your family, well you might want to consider travelling a different career path.

I have more important things to consider right now. I need to find Gaunt, and stop him before he kills my son. I've avoided going to that point in time, but now it's clear that I'm the only one who can change the way all this pans out - of course it does beg the question, what happens when I stop Gaunt from killing my son?

The letter I sent myself says nothing about it, it just tells me what to do with Juju - so obviously at some point later, I'm going to go and set up that rescue. Before that I'm going to go and take on Gaunt. What happens if I fail? If that means I don't set up the rescue, then I can't go and do this. If I can't go and do this then does the rescue happen some other way? I'm getting tied up in knots thinking about this stuff.

The light is fading at the old house when I get there. I open the door and creep inside. Passing the living room, I see Luke sat in front of the television, bathed in its cold light. Eliza is out, I know. I remember every detail of this night, it's etched on my brain like the markings on a tombstone. I head up the stairs to wait for Gaunt. Joshua is in his nursery, sleeping in his cot. I peer over him as he sleeps, the top of his head poking out of the covers and his best bear next to him - his fingers squeeze bear's hand in rhythm with his breath. I back out of the room, by habit really, I can't wake him up from here. Then I head back downstairs to the kitchen.

The big carving knife in the block will do nicely. I prise open a small hole in the membrane between worlds and reach through, pulling the knife slowly from the block. Unexpectedly it slips, and the whole block slides off the counter with a crash. I remember just in time how this had happened - and withdrew my arm and the knife just in time as Luke comes running into the kitchen to find the knives all over the floor. He looks around uneasily before picking them up, returning the block to the counter. Before he leaves the kitchen he checks that the back door is locked, and satisfied that it's secure, he returns to his spot on the couch.

I breathe a sigh of relief and head back up the stairs to stand guard. He will be here soon, and I'll be waiting for him. I finger the knife in my hand, and consider that I have never actually inflicted direct violence on anyone before, well apart from that day in the schoolyard. I've never inflicted direct violence on someone using a weapon. I always found in horror movies that of all the elaborate weapons the psycho killers used, the one that always got to me most was the knife. Everything else seemed so extravagant - the axe, the chainsaw, the lawnmower in Braindead.

But the knife, there was something so mundane about it, and I think that's what made it seem such a terrible weapon. The sound of a movie stabbing - thunk thunk thunk. We've all accidentally cut ourselves, so it's easy to imagine what it might feel like - just let your imagination amplify that pain from a cut finger, multiply out the horror of your blood leaking out into a torrent. It would always make me shudder. I heard quiet steps on the stairs, a creak - saw the shadow on the stairwell, just like Nosferatu. Gaunt was here. He stepped around the bend of the stairwell, stopping when he saw me. I raised the knife.

"You're more resourceful than I thought, Mister Loupe."

"Give it up, Gaunt. I won't let you do this."

"You don't understand the danger the boy poses, I take no pleasure from this." - the gleam in his beady eye said otherwise.

"Somehow I don't believe you."

"Trust is a difficult thing to earn."

"Especially from someone you've tied up and beaten to a pulp."

"Nonetheless, you really need to step aside. Your vision in this is clouded. The boy is an abomination."

"They used to say that about women so they could have a little bonfire."

"Sometimes, they were right. They just got a little overzealous."

"You're wrong about Joshua."

"We're not, and you know it. Now let me pass, Mister Loupe", through gritted teeth.

"Fat chance. You want to get to Joshua, you have to get through me."

"Yes. Very well. I believe the appropriate phrase is... shall we dance?"

He lunges forward at me, like a striking snake, and I slash out with the knife. It's pretty obvious that I don't know what I'm doing, but I have the advantage of being armed in a narrow corridor - he has to get through me to get into the nursery. His arm comes up, and I inflict a deep cut on his arm. Gaunt bellows, blood blooming into his sleeve from a neat wound in his wrist. He drops, and tries to go under the knife, but there is nowhere for him to go. He claws and bites at me like a rabid dog, nearly unbalancing me, but as I stagger into the wall I feel something twist out of place in my shoulder, a blinding pain that explodes like fireworks through my nervous system.

Gaunt sees his opportunity and breaks through for the door, but I manage to reverse my grip on the knife and bring it down in a swift arc, embedding it in his back - I feel a moment's resistance as the blade meets his flesh, but then it slides in as if it was oiled. Gaunt decks out. I spin, and straddle his prone form, the knife rising and falling to an inaudible beat. Thunk thunk thunk. Just like the movies.

He lies there in a spreading pool of blood. None of it has the drama I imagined. The whole thing was over so quickly, almost in an instant - and I am struck by how ordinary it felt, not like I could go around stabbing people left, right and centre - ordinary as in cheap, common. I feel exhilarated, feel sick to my stomach. I drop the bloodied knife, and roll Gaunt over onto his back - kneeling on his chest. His eyes bulge out of his face, staring at nothing with brutal intensity. Here is my invisible monster, and I have slain the beast. Now hopefully things can be very different, can't they? Maybe not for me, but for Luke, and for Joshua.

I stand, and step over Gaunt's corpse and into the nursery. My arm, its shoulder dislocated I think, hangs at my side - a dull throbbing pain punctuated by a sharp stabbing agony with every step. Joshua is stood in his cot, illuminated by a patch of light from the open door. His face wears an expression that should never exist on a child, an expression of years and an expression of boiling vengeful hatred.

The shadows coalesce around him, rise from his skin like black smoke. Then I realise that I was wrong. The view from beyond reality is like a two way mirror in an interrogation room - from one side you can see only what happens in the room itself, but the view from the other side is more than the sum of its parts - the act of observing unseen changes the context of what's happening in there, making the truth bubble to the surface.

When I used to look at Joshua I just saw an ordinary baby boy, but from here the truth was evident. Whatever Joshua was, he wasn't ordinary. He truly was a horror, an abomination - and I'd just killed the one other person who could have dealt with him in the only way possible. Besides, of course he had to die - his death was inevitable, destined. Just because I was here now - I could remember it, which meant it had already happened. I got so tied up in thinking about saving him that I didn't consider that obvious fact. You can't unmake history, you can only observe it.

"Daddy", Joshua growled, and I nearly threw up.

INTERLUDE EIGHT

A Routine Checkup With Angela Docent, DDS

If there was one thing that annoyed Angela Docent, it was people missing appointments, or turning up late. For Angela, her punctuality was a point of pride - and she expected others to maintain the same high standards she did. Some might consider her prissy, but she considered tardiness to be unbearably rude. It was the lack of consideration for others that really got to her - if she was even running a minute late, she would be painfully aware that other people would then be forced to wait for her.

It didn't matter if she'd been up late on the forums with the others, she followed a strict daily routine, designed to make sure that everything happened when it was supposed to happen. Her alarm went off at 5.30, allowing precisely three presses of the snooze button before she rose at six o'clock and jumped in the shower. She brushed her teeth for exactly two minutes. By 6.30, she was eating breakfast, which also allowed for her to scan the news headlines, and make sure there were no traffic snarl-ups on her route to work. It was important to check these things to allow her to make adjustments. Whatever happened, Angela Docent always arrived at the practice at exactly nine in the morning, on the dot, no exceptions.

But, she checked her diary, Alex Jones thought he was special. Alex Jones and both her previous appointments thought that the normal niceties, the basic consideration for others that greased the wheels of commerce and society didn't apply to him. She slammed the diary shut. Alex was the straw that broke the camel's back today, and she sat giving serious thought to recommending an unnecessary root canal when he finally showed up.

She sat and waiting, looking at the clock periodically. If the next client was late, there was a good chance she'd set the surgery on fire before going on a crazed drilling rampage around the city. She imagined there would be plenty of odontophobes fleeing in panic as some giant godzilla dentist stomped around smashing buildings like so many rotten molars, swinging an enormous drill to smash their tiny running bodies aside.

Of course it was to expected. Angela was well aware of the darker forces at work in the world, the lizard-people who were sitting in the seats of power. Each of them lorded it over the remaining humans, living in their thrall like so many sheep being led to the slaughterhouse. Not Angela though, she believed that knowledge was power, and lived every day prepared for the day when the lizards made their final moves, checkmating the remainder of humanity of all time. She was pretty sure that they were monitoring her internet communications, but that was the only way she had to stay in touch with the other members of the resistance. In the meantime, she had to keep her head down, look as ordinary as she could. Blend in, that was the watchword.

Angela didn't notice as an invisible hand nudged the minute hand on her clock, just enough to tip her over the edge.

Her reverie was interrupted by her receptionist buzzing in her next patient. She looked at the clock again - fifteen minutes late, typical. In he walked, bold as brass, as if he'd done nothing wrong. As if he didn't think her time wasn't as valuable as his. Then he popped himself in the chair without so much as a by-your-leave. Without so much as an apology for his inexcusable behaviour. She held back a twitch of rage and walked over to him. He knew the drill, and opened wide for his examination.

That was when Angela Docent saw the smile behind his smile, and realised that she had one of them in her chair. He only let the mask slip for a fraction of a second, but that was all it took - once seen, it couldn't be unseen. She'd seen videos of course, grainy footage posted to YouTube.

The videos were compelling, especially once you knew what you were looking for. Naturally the lizard overlords allowed them to be published. They were clever, they knew that to censor the information would only add to its credibility. As it was, most people thought of the true believers as kooks and nutjobs. Today, though, they would regret their overconfidence, because Angela knew what she was looking for. Forewarned, forearmed, and ready to act in the service of all humanity. She had one of the lizards here, in her grasp, and the opportunity to get the evidence.

Clearly this one was overconfident in its disguise. Angela went through the motions of an examination, and suggested that there was a problem in one of the patient's molars. It would require a deeper examination, and she offered a little sedation just to make it easier on him. He accepted the laughing gas with no qualms, and it took him down just enough. She made a mental note that the lizards were not impervious to the effects of nitrous oxide - it was all information that might prove valuable once the war began. As he relaxed on the chair, she looked around to find something suitable to restrain him.

He seemed unconcerned, in a nitrous daze, as she tied him to the chair with electrical cord. First his legs, then his arms. She locked the door, and returned to loop the flex around his neck. She didn't want him moving his head around as she unmasked him. It was at this point he realised what was going on. Angela would have to work fast - she started the video camera on her phone and reached for the scalpel. His screams would soon fetch others of his kind to try to prevent her striking this blow for humanity, to stop her getting the irrefutable evidence out there once and for all.

The first incision, a deep cut down the left hand side of the face as the doorknob rattled and worried voices asked if everything was OK. Then the right side, cutting as far in as she could, to get through the layers of the lizard's disguise. The lizard was screaming now, and the attempts to get through the door became more frantic. It was hard to focus with the video camera while doing the job one handed, but

Angela figured she didn't need to do too neat a job to get the mask off.

A final cut, sawing across the forehead, then she just had to jam her fingers into the cut just so and pull as hard as she could. The disguise was well attached, but Angela put all her strength into it, making sure she captured the alien lizard's disgusting face on her phone video. They were trying to beat the door down now, so she dropped the scalpel and let the loose mask flop to one side. She turned to her phone, and she was still waiting for the video to upload when the door burst open. Her practice partner, Dr. Gupta's horrified face said it all. The truth was finally out.

The video got over a hundred thousand views before it was taken down for violating the terms of service.

CHAPTER EIGHTEEN

I Am The Dog Who Arranges The Blocks

Our current situation could be compared to a game of tetris, because eventually we're going to run out of ammunition, and that point those blocks are going to be falling faster and faster. You can always spot a long time tetris player - they're haunted by the knowledge that no matter how good they are, they can never actually win, just survive longer than everyone else.

Failure in Tetris in inevitable, and all you can do is delay the point at which you're going to get buried. Who would have thought that the most addictive video game ever created could also be such an effective metaphor for life?

I'm not sure if Boris and Karloff are the greatest mercenaries in the history of the world, or if the Authority's men are suffering from a terrible case of stormtrooper syndrome, but things aren't looking half as bleak as they should. Despite what sounds like enough firepower out in the corridor to support a minor coup in any number of failed soviet states - they are taking advantage of our well covered position and the bottlenecked approach to our hidey-hole to lay down very effective suppressing fire.

The bodies were certainly piling up out there. It gives me cause to wonder... what happens to the dead when they die? You hope that once you shuffle off your mortal coil that the veil will be lifted and you're granted access-all-areas to the mysteries of the universe. Unfortunately, that's not the case - you just find yourself in the same old situation, not knowing really who you are, or what to do, or what happens next. Sorry to be the bearer of bad news, but there you have it. I've seen people fade out of this plane of existence, and I've seen people be violently thrust from it as well - I have no idea what happens in either case. Do they go the same way? Perhaps there is some new level of purgatory for the dead who are violently killed again? I hope not, because it's looking more likely by the second that I'm going to go there.

Then the click of an empty chamber and a curse from Boris. Karloff reaches for the cell door and slams it shut. It's a heavy metal door, but lacks any way of barring it from the inside - I guess you can't have prisoners locking themselves in. There's the sound of running feet approaching in the corridor, and Boris tugs the door open again, and rolls a grenade out, slamming the door shut again. It's an interesting sound, the sound of a grenade going off - your ears kind of shut down to try to keep the noise out, and the resulting effect is kind of a muffled crump, like an enormous cardboard box being violently squashed. That might sound quite inoffensive, but judging from the screams outside, it's not so good if you're inside the box at the time.

It's got very quiet now. Clearly our friends out there have decided to pause for a cuppa and a bit of a rethink. Boris opens the door a crack to take a peek. The corridor is filled with smoke and blood, the dead and dying strewn about. Not a living soul is visible. Then a figure steps into the end of the corridor, and start to walk towards us. His wings are raised, and brush against the walls as he walks - the feathers look down-soft, but scrape along the old plaster like steel nails, leaving trailing gouges behind them. Karloff pops his clip to take a look - just a couple of bullets left. He nods to Boris, who swings the door wide. Karloff stands in the doorway, raises his pistol and fires.

The shot hits Nathaniel in the shoulder. He twitches backward slightly, but doesn't stop walking towards us. Karloff squeezes off his last two rounds, both direct hits, and both about as effective as a tissue-paper trampoline. The men look at each other and then look at me, shrugging - the universal language for "that's it then". They throw their guns on the floor, raise their hands in surrender, and step out into the corridor as Nathaniel bears down on us. Big mistake.

As he approaches he raises his hands toward them, and both men drop to their knees as if in supplication. The smile never leaves Nathaniel's face as he places one hand atop each man's head, and then grips and twists. Their heads come off real easy, and the angel stands there for a moment letting the blood rain down around him before underarm bowling the heads away behind him. I'm stood at the back of the cell, watching through the open door, as he steps through, squeezing his wings through behind him. Then he stands there, just smiling, as the door swings shut behind him.

"This is getting ridiculous. What have you done? Have you any idea what kind of power you are toying with here, dog? Do you have no clue what I am?"

"Well", I figure at this point, I might as well enjoy myself before he plucks all my legs off, "Covered in blood... wings... are you a used sanitary towel? I admire your commitment to the role, but you're never going to get those stains out."

He opens his mouth and roars at me. He might have a human face, and a vaguely human body, but this thing is less human than even me. And if you hadn't noticed so far... I'm a dog. Spittle flies from his mouth, and the air fills with dense harmonics that would have made my fur stand on end if I'd had any, gooseflesh crawls. Of course, I'm never one to miss the opportunity for one of the classic zingers.

"Somebody needs a mint."

"Listen, you little shit. You're going to tell me where Loupe has gone or you're going to get far worse than your two friends did. They were lucky, they got the quick version, but I can make your death last a very long, exceptionally unpleasant, and ludicrously painful time."

"Wow, I thought Gaunt was bad, but you're something else."

"You ain't seen nothing yet."

"Well how about you let me go, I go, and we call it a draw? Really, I'm just an innocent bystander here so perhaps we could consider a deal like that? You let me walk out of here entirely unharmed, I don't say anything to anyone about anything, and if Loupe shows his face I'll give you a call? Just give me your digits and we'll go from there. I can go and grow my lovely glossy-ish coat back, find a hot bitch settle down and make puppies, afterlive happily ever after...?"

I'm babbling now, because let's face it, I'm pretty much screwed at this point - Loupe knew it, and I knew it before I came in here. This is, unfortunately for me, all part of the plan. Loupe had explained it all to me back at Wong's Wosh And Winse, and every bit of it was unstoppable, inevitable. This is the point in the tetris game where a couple of blocks get out of line, and then a couple of blocks fall that have nowhere to go. The wall starts to develop gaps, and the top of the pile is suddenly a lot closer to the top of the screen than it was a minute ago. I grip the letter from Loupe, and take a deep breath, remembering what he wrote, feeling the words through the scrunch of paper in my left paw.

"Juju, I feel partly responsible for this, and I'm sorry you're having to do this thing - I wouldn't ask you if I could do it myself, but we've all got our destinies, and mine lies elsewhere. You've been a good friend, the best friend - and when

206

the end comes, I want you to remember that what you're doing is way bigger than the afterlives of a couple of schmucks like us. We've talked about what happens when the dead die before, and we never had any answers - but if there's any justice you'll end up somewhere better than this place, somewhere better than the old terra vitae, even. The Authority has to be stopped, though, they're interfering with the real world - they're stopping people from living out their lives the way they should be lived - according to the whims of chance, and the random dice rolls of the universe. We don't even have a choice, the paths we're travelling are inevitable and unavoidable, but untold lives will be freed of the same curse when you do this. I don't think we'll meet again, but I hope you find something better. I'm sorry I told you that you would walk out of this, but Nathaniel isn't going to fold. He's going to call you out. Sorry again, but this is the way things have to play out. Love you, man. Loupe."

The game continues regardless of how carefully I'm watching, or not. A T-shape block falls, and I'm not paying attention. It lands sideways. The first gap appears in my wall.

Nathaniel takes a step toward me, I cower against the wall - every instinct in my body wants me to get away, refuses to accept that it's over. We knew this moment was coming, and Loupe had talked me through it in painstaking detail, the simple plan to take down the Authority, to take down Nathaniel, but actually here and now, the practical test, was a very different situation to the theoretical discussion back at the launderette.

A left handed S block. I try to slide it in under the gap, but miss. Another gap, and the first one now inaccessible. The bricks start to fall faster.

The angel smiles, the kind of smile that says your skin will soon be a lampshade and your bones will be toothpicks. Another step forward, and he's towering over me. I look at him, and reach for the zip on my jacket, slide it down - the way time has slowed, I feel almost like a stripper, like some bass-heavy sex music should be playing as I draw Nathaniel into my web of seduction-for-a-price. C'mere baby, I got something to show you.

A straight four, and I screw up the rotation, it lands flat across a big hole, leaving a cavern in the centre of the wall. I could try to save it, but the relentless series of bricks will always win in the end. There's only one realistic option now, at least one where I get to choose how the game ends. I just have to stop struggling, let the blocks fall, one at a time. They can stack up pretty high before it's all over. Here comes one, and another, each on top of the previous, balancing impossibly, defying the laws of physics. You can kind of argue that choosing to lose is a form of winning.

His hands reach down for me, and as he grabs my arms, he sees that I have another jacket under the one I just undid. A natty little waistcoat, with a fetching pinstripe in a rather handsome grey-brown moleskin shade. More notable than its fashion qualities, however, are the fact that it's stuffed with electronics and enough C4 to demolish a moderately sized youth centre. I drop the letter from Loupe, letting it drift to the floor, and then point to my other paw, holding it up to show Nathaniel what I'm holding on to.

"And they call this a dead man's switch. You know what that is? I think they also call it a fait accompli, you overgrown part-seagull son of a bitch."

The final block falls. It's a square, and it drives itself onto the top of the pile, though it doesn't have any space to fall into. It always ends this way.

Nathaniel has two options - let me go and hope he gets out of the way, or that I don't drop the switch, or kill me, in which case I'll release the switch anyway. He's still spinning blocks even though the game is already over. Indecision flickers over his face, and I take the moment to choose for him. I let go of the switch, and an inferno blossoms out from my lovely waistcoat.

The concussive force of the explosion pretty much vapourises me, apart from a few fragments that have no idea what's going on anyway. Nathaniel is overwhelmed by its destructive force as well, torn into a thousand thousand burning, screaming fragments - beyond that, a considerable portion of sublevel seven of the Authority building takes a reckless amount of damage, causing portions of the construction to collapse, and severely ruining the day of a not insignificant number of Authority employees.

As for what happens when the dead die? Well I guess this is where I get to find out.

CHAPTER NINETEEN

Scary Monsters, Super Creeps

I stared at Joshua, this creature I'd loved, and he stared back. His eyes were filled with coal dust, a malevolent force set on bending the world to its will, to force the world to its knees before him. I could see the future stretching out behind this point, and the future was not bright. Even now, Joshua was an apex predator in everything but body, and if he was allowed to reach maturity there would be no hope for humanity - and since I'd created him, there would be no hope for me - if I let him live, I was surely damned.

Luke paused, reached for the remote and muted the television for a moment. Did he hear a cry? His breath was held in his throat. Nothing, he must have imagined it, a sound in the background of the movie. He hit the volume button, and relaxed, grabbing another crisp from the bowl. Cheese and onion, absolutely the best flavour.

I took a step forward, and the child (I had to exert every bit of willpower to not think of him... it... as Joshua) raised its hands, as if to ward me away. "I deserve to live. Just turn and go. Haven't you done enough, Daddy? Wasn't it bad enough that you stole my life from me, that you made me this way? Now you've come to finish the job? Is that it?

You think I'm evil - but what have I done? Nothing. Not compared to you, not compared to the things I've done". I didn't know what he was talking about, not then. I gritted my teeth, and prepared to do the worst thing I had ever done, the culmination of a catalogue of misdeeds. Perhaps he was right - I've done so many terrible things, unforgivable things. But I don't think I'm evil - though I don't think anyone ever does, we all justify our actions however we can. We don't have a choice.

Again. Luke froze mid-crunch, and hit pause again. A cry from upstairs. He'd hoped Joshua was down for the night, but it looked like it was going to be another one of those unstoppable nights of the baby going off the bendy end. He sighed, put the remaining half a crisp back in the bowl, and got up from the sofa, heading for the stairs.

I told myself to get a grip - this was the child trying to get under my skin, doing what it had to in order to survive. It briefly crossed my mind that I could just let it live - but I knew that it all came down to this moment, and like Gaunt, this moment had already happened, and so already had to happen. It wanted to get into my head, wanted to fulfil the destiny it saw for itself - unfortunately for it, some destinies trump others. I took a step forward, and it stumbled backward in its cot. Then I reached across for my useless arm, and forced my shoulder back into its socket as best I could.

Luke reached the nursery door. Jacob was yelling fit to burst now - blue murder. He pushed the door open, and saw Joshua at the rear corner of his cot, eyes and mouth wide, bright red and screaming like Death and all his horsemen were coming for him. He knew that it was probably nothing, trapped wind or just a bad dream, but whenever he heard Jacob like that - a part of him was terrified that something was seriously wrong this time. A terrible illness, a bone caught in the throat. Who knew? He took a step forward to pick him up, to comfort him, but something got there before him.

I grabbed the child, lifting it up in the air. Its hands scratched at my face, pulled at my hair, and it arched its back and kicked out, doing everything it could to disengage from my grip.

I'd felt Joshua do the same thing when trying to resist a nappy change, and the sensation brought those moments of fatherhood flooding back - but I had to focus, had to do what I was here to do.

Luke screamed in horror as Joshua launched vertically from his cot, and hung in the air before him, screaming and bucking against some kind of invisible force that held up in defiance of gravity. He stumbled backward as his baby swung around towards him, levitating through the air. He gasped for breath as all the years of fear culminated in a moment when those fears finally came true. Staggering forward, he grabbed for his son, catching him in his hands.

Luke couldn't see me, but he grabbed the child, and suddenly we were forced into a tug of war. The child-thing was hissing and spitting at me like a feral creature, possessed by devils, and Luke was pulling with all his might, but I was more powerful. Luke's fingers slipped, and the child fell into my grasp, momentum swinging it around and into the wall.

Luke screamed in horror as his child was flung into the wall by the force in the nursery, there was a sickening crack, and blood flew, spattering the walls with forensic evidence. He ran forward and tried to grab the boy again.

The details don't matter now. You know what happened. I remember it from Luke's point of view, and I never want to remember it from mine. I did what I had to do, that's all, and even though Jacob was... what he was, he was still mine. My abomination. My monster. I looked at him, and lowered him back into his cot, where the sheets absorbed the worst of it, and the shadow that lived within him dissipated into the air.

Luke tried to save him, but when the ambulance arrived and the paramedics came into the room, they knew there was no chance. One of them took Luke downstairs while the other one called the police. They kept talking to him quietly, in hushed tones, tried to keep him calm. He was numb anyway, and when the police came to take him he didn't offer any resistance.

INTERLUDE NINE

An Unfortunate Gig Cancellation For Dennis Glew

The pain was excruciating. There was something so special about toothache, how a problem so localised could send rivers of pain seemingly through your whole body. Talk about a design flaw, one of the most fragile parts of the human body being apparently wired directly into your spine, a direct line of screaming agony to the core of the nervous system. He was going to get it sorted today though, and just in time - the Snopes had a big gig at the Skeleton Key tonight, the first one in a while. Rumour was that there were going to be some A&R guys there. He'd heard such rumours before, and took them with a pinch of salt, but you couldn't help some tiny part of you hoping that this time it might be true.

Dennis Glew had managed to get an emergency appointment. He'd been dealing with this tooth for the last six months, filling the cavity using some emergency home dental repair kit he'd read about online. This was what oral care had come to, people having to buy kits to fill their own teeth. There was probably a song in that somewhere - it wouldn't be long before ordinary folks had to perform their own emergency appendectomies without anaesthetic the way this country was going.

He found himself stood outside the surgery of Docent and Gupta, amid a chaotic scene of police tape and squad cars, like something off the telly. A woman in a white coat was being herded into the back of a police van and officers manning the perimeter told him in no uncertain terms that emergency appointment or no, he wasn't receiving any dental treatment today. One of the younger coppers told him that he should be glad he hadn't been in there, out of the corner of his mouth. Dennis had no idea what had happened, and trudged away dejected as a body bag was wheeled out of the surgery door and straight into the coroner's van.

He grabbed his mobile and started making calls. Nothing. It wasn't even like he wasn't willing to pay for the treatment, but there was simply no room at the inn. Everyone told him to take painkillers and try again tomorrow - but painkillers weren't doing anything to touch this, as his unhappy tooth periodically nail-gunned his jaw, head and spinal column. Eventually an emergency dental helpline told him he could go and wait in line at an emergency surgery on Bokeh Street, though there were no guarantees he would be seen, he'd just have to take a number and take his chances. Fine.

It was a fair hike across town, but he got to the surgery, took a ticket and sat down amongst an astonishing line-up of the dregs of humanity. Dennis wasn't a snob by any means, but this place made him feel like he'd wandered onto the set of the Jeremy Kyle show. He kept his head down, took his phone out of his pocket, and fiddled around with it, waiting for his number to come up. The display on the wall said twenty four. He looked at his ticket. Sixty three. It was going to be a long day. He gritted his teeth, and immediately regretted it as the bad one complained loudly.

The old woman next to him muttered constantly, a stream of words that no-one's grandmother should know. Dennis wondered what she could possibly be doing here, such an ancient crone surely didn't have any teeth left for a dentist to do anything with? Maybe she was having her gums polished or something. She smelled bad as well, a less-than-alluring combination of cough medicine, sherry, and old urine. The receptionist called for ticket number thirty two. He pulled the ticket out of his pocket and checked again. Still sixty three.

As he put the ticket back in his pocket, he failed to notice that it caught on a seam, leaving it hanging slightly out into the world, making a break for freedom. Then it leaped into open space, as if lightly tugged by invisible fingers, and allowed to float away, drifting into a snug and safe space behind his chair. The trainered foot of a spotty youth with an abscess landed on it, and the ticket clung on to the sole to make its escape, like a prisoner of war hanging on to the bottom of a transport truck for grim life.

The interminable waiting continued, and Dennis entered a strange fugue state, time seeming to flex around him until he was jolted back to reality by the announcement of his number. Glorious, magical sixty three. He jumped up, and reached to his pocket for the ticket. Hold on. He checked the other pocket. Nothing. Frantically he scrambled through all of his pockets, spilling plectrums, receipts and small change but the ticket, that ticket he wouldn't have exchanged for one of Willy Wonka's golden tickets, was gone.

He pleaded with the receptionist, but she insisted that no-one would be treated without a proper ticket - otherwise where would we be? Anarchy, she said, refusing to open the floodgates on Dennis's dental revolution. He went through all seven stages of grief while stood at that reception desk, finally accepting that his only option was to take another number. One hundred and twenty one. The receptionist pointed out that he probably had more chance of his tooth spontaneously repairing itself than seeing a dentist today. She suggested he go home, and come back earlier tomorrow.

The pain was worse now than ever. Grudgingly, Dennis accepted that there was no way he could sing a note tonight, A&R men or not - unless there was a new fashion for frontmen who sang songs while crying like little girls, they were going to have to cancel. He grabbed his phone and called the promoter at the Skeleton Key. They were very understanding - these things happen - and they said they would find some other local act to step into the breach and fill the slot.

CHAPTER TWENTY

Broken Britain Going For Gold In The Grief Olympiad

What happened after that? Well, Luke told the police what happened, and they didn't believe him. Soon the story was in the papers, and although no-one source released enough information to make Luke a target, it wasn't a puzzle to tax even the more simple of minds. Facebook, being the magical haven of consequence free rabid mob screaming that it was, soon had thousands upon thousands of people who had got on board with the modern day hobby of waving cyber-pitchforks about - all of them were in groups saying how I should be strung up, tortured and strung up, and split open, tortured, and strung up.

I didn't know about any of this at the time. I was incarcerated, kept in solitary confinement - I was told this was for my own safety, that there was "considerable public anger". I wasn't changing my story, and I was examined by doctors and psychiatrists, by criminologists and forensics experts. I went through three different lawyers in the next two weeks, all of whom decided there was no way they could come out of defending me looking good - I was something of a career killer, it seemed. The guards in the prison didn't seem particularly concerned with my well being beyond their basic job of keeping me alive for the trial. The meals came cold and late, and I had a suspicion that they were waiting expectantly for the guilty verdict in the courts so they could begin the daily beatings that no-one would ever need to know about.

I told all of them the same story, and that story was the truth as I understood it then. It wasn't me. It was an invisible monster. Yes, I knew how that sounded. No, I didn't think it was some part of my mind trying to deny what I'd done, that I'd snapped and beaten my son to death. No, that simply wasn't possible, I knew what I'd seen. Soon enough, though, I started to doubt my own mind. My memories turned against me as they battled the twin forces of reason and logic. Perhaps they were right, perhaps I was insane. Perhaps I'd actually done this terrible thing and I was subconsciously editing my memories to blame this "invisible monster" when in fact if I could have seen that invisible monster all I would have seen was a mirror of myself. And in a way, that was true.

Eliza came to visit me once. She looked like she hadn't slept since she'd got home that night to find the police waiting for her and me gone, and Joshua covered up all the way to the top. The strength that had run through her like a river had simply dried up, and the cracks that I'd made in her had finally opened up. She nearly spoke several times, but thought better of it.

She sat on the other side of the table and stared at me, her eyes dark and hollow. I didn't know what to say, and I think she'd already made her mind up anyway. Finally the darkness that she'd fought to keep me safe from, that she'd given up everything to take on, had risen up like some kind of terrible inferno, incinerating everything that she'd loved in one night of insane cruelty. Then she left.

It was two weeks later when the trap was sprung. It turned out that the guards transporting me to my trial were keen members of the facebook hate club, and instead of doing their job they transported me to a meeting that had been set up. A crowd gathered around the prison truck, shaking it, jostling it on its suspension. The baying of the mob started to sound less like individual voices, more like the terrifying howls of a single alien organism, a murderous hive mind come to the earth to feed its insatiable blood lust. I couldn't see out of the blacked-out windows though. I thought we were arriving at the court. I couldn't have been more mistaken.

The rear doors of the truck were flung, nearly torn open, and there they were like a scene from Night Of The Living Dead. I had nowhere to run as they grabbed at me, dragged me out into the field where they'd gathered. Ahead of me, I saw the crude gallows some of them had built, and for a moment I thought I saw Eliza in the crowd, but then she was gone. I was screaming now, a lone voice of terror tossed about in an ocean of murderous hate.

They showed some degree of control, though - they'd been organised, a pack of dogs muzzled by a higher power. That didn't stop blows raining down on me as I was dragged to the podium, but it kept me from being killed until they were ready. I was pushed up onto the crude platform, and the noose was thrown around my neck, pulled tight. A cable tie held my hands behind my back, my wrists twisted roughly but effectively.

Then I saw her again, Eliza, moving through the crowd as they parted around her - the perfect character for her role, the vengeful mother. She joined me on the platform, and I tried to move towards her, to tell her I hadn't done it, to try to explain. I was rewarded by one of the flanking prison officers hitting me in the mouth with a brick, smashing my jaw. My vision swam as I choked on blood and fragments of teeth. Then Eliza looked at me without a shred of pity in her eyes. "You killed an angel.", she said, with no idea how right she would be, and pulled the lever. I dropped, until the rope ran out.

I never saw what happened after that, it was the drop that finished me, but I know from seeing the news later. The crowd surged at the platform, and literally tore me to pieces. Britain hadn't seen anything like it since medieval times. Three people were killed in the crush, trampled underfoot by the crowd pouring out its rage into one act of violence. Looking back, I don't think I was even relevant to it - it could have been anyone. I just happened to be in the wrong place at the wrong time.

Soon after that, once I'd started to adjust to the reality of my new situation, I got my job at the Authority, and met the JuJu Puppy - the rest, as they say, is history. Or the future. In a way, it's all the same thing.

CHAPTER TWENTY-ONE

Tying Up The Loose Ends

After JuJu, Boris, and Karloff had left the Wosh And Winse to rescue me from the Authority, I turned to The Mouse, and handed him the briefcase containing JuJu's three million.

"There you go. Make sure you look after their families."

"Men like that don't have families, I'm afraid. Don't worry, their eyes are more open than you might think - they know the risks. I'll look after it for 'em, just in case."

"There is no just in case. Everything will happen just like I've told you."

"In which case, I'll enjoy it on their behalf. Three million seems like a small price for two lives."

"So what are you going to do now?"

"Business is business, I'll just get back to it - even if you're right, even if the Authority is going down... something will take its place. Systems persist, you know. Who knows, maybe it'll even be me - I could be the Mayor Of The Land Of The Dead."

"You don't seem the type for elected officialdom."

"Who said anything about an election?"

With that, The Mouse turned and left, leaving me with the Wongs. Each had taken a position equidistant from me, putting me at the centre of a triangle with one of their moist heads at each vertex. They were bobbing excitedly, and closed in like hyenas - sniffing at me like I was some kind of delicious meal.

"Back off a bit, you're making me nervous."

"Weir mere leigh tea sting. Sofa hewn you flay version this life."

"I'm a new flavour?"

"Years. Nod sin won lick yew beef oar."

"What do you mean?"

But I knew what they meant. Whatever I was, it wasn't what I'd thought. I wasn't strictly even one of the dead, because I wasn't even human. I was a glitch in the system, a cuckoo who knocked someone else's eggs out of the nest and moved myself in in their place. I lived a stolen human life - not the most ordinary of human lives, but nonetheless it was mine. I took a place in reality meant for someone else, some parasite feeding off the wrinkle in space-time I inhabit.

Don't hate me though, I'm only doing this to survive - if nothing else, that's an instinct we all share. Besides, I don't think everything I've done is that bad. Like any really successful parasite, I give as well as take. I'm not much enjoying talking about myself in these terms - cuckoo, parasite... whatever I am, I still feel human, because I've lived as one of you, and I've died as one of you - I've felt human fear, and I've experienced human love. I've been a son, and a husband, and a father, so who's to say that I'm not at least sort of human?

Of course, I'm not - no more than a cuckoo is a starling, but you get my point. I've done the things that humans do, and felt the things they feel. As far as I was concerned, up to now, I was just as human as the rest of them, and if I'm right, I've done that more than any of you ever will, because I have to be Luke and Loupe over and again in order to stay alive. There's just a couple more things left to do, and then it's time to go all the way back to the start, just wind that clock back.

Ha. Cuckoo clock.

INTERLUDE TEN

A Night At The Skeleton Key With Eliza Morgan

Eliza's internet connection had stopped working, so she had no idea that The Snopes had pulled out of that night's gig at The Skeleton Key. She'd been looking forward to it for the last couple of months, and was ready for a good night. She'd assumed the connection problem was one of the usual quirks of the up and down service from her cable provider, and didn't worry about it too much. She had other things to think about, like choosing an outfit, making sure Sam was ready to be picked up on the way down. She never bothered to check, and didn't see that some mischievous pixie had unplugged the cable from her router. A good job too, because if she'd known the Snopes weren't going to be on, she'd probably have canned the whole night out.

Sam was ready for once, but Eliza spent ten minutes waiting outside her house with the meter running while she tried to find her mobile phone. She was sure she'd left it on the table, but it took a few phone calls and careful listening to the ringtone to find it under the fridge. Sam figured she must have accidentally knocked off while rushing about trying to get something to eat, ready to absorb the alcohol. That delay, fortunately, meant the Eliza and Sam missing the departure of Richie and Dean from the Skeleton Key. If they'd turned up on time, they wouldn't have bothered staying, going instead to another gig in another pub.

The Skeleton Key was pretty full, and as Sam took the first of many toilet visits, Eliza went to the bar. A carefully nudged elbow drew her eyes to the left instead of the right, and she laid eyes on Luke for the first time. That first look meant she saw Luke's best profile, and just as he was standing under fortunate lighting that make him look his best. She didn't realise it, but her subconscious brain, right down on the lizard level, clocked him and appraised him and filed him under "potentially interesting". In situations like this, even the smallest of factors can make a difference. Unaware, she continued to the bar, and ordered drinks - a couple of vodka and cokes, and a pair of sambucas to get things started on the right foot.

She saw Sam working her way through the crowd to her, and carefully picked up the four drinks to make the rendezvous. Focused on her destination, she didn't see the hipster stumbling backwards towards her from the starboard side. Or at least, she wouldn't have done if one of the guitar cables plugged into the waiting onstage amps hadn't somehow chosen that moment to become slightly unplugged, filling the room with an unpleasant buzz of feedback, and drawing her attention in that direction. She sidestepped the stumbling hipster, and just in time - a dousing in sticky drinks would probably have been enough to make her decide to sack this night off before it started.

The first band took to the stage. One song in and Luke swept past her. He would have bumped into her, causing him to lose points in her lizard-brain scorecard, but fortunately a gentle push applied to a couple of other members of the crowd opened up alternative routes through the crush, routes that Luke followed to make sure he didn't come into contact with Eliza yet, not in any way that would reduce his potential standing with her. Things were getting harder to control now, I'd painted all the broad strokes, but now I was filling in the finer details. Every moment was a potential disaster, a potentially wrong turn.

The band were definitely not pushing Eliza's buttons, but she was tolerating them for the moment. Sadly, their performance started to degrade as tiny invisible tweaks on the tuning pegs of the guitars caused their instruments to go slightly out of tune - not a lot, but enough to turn the tolerable into the offensive to someone who's heard enough music to know the difference. Eliza tugged on Sam's sleeve to attract her attention over the din. As Sam turned, she pulled her cigarettes out of her bag, tapped them, and pointed at the exit to the beer garden. Sam nodded agreement, and they wandered outside.

They had a cigarette, and this was the big moment, the turning point. I was willing Luke to step in, to make some kind of move, and he wasn't stepping up to the plate - of course he didn't know that he was looking through a narrowing window of opportunity as he stood there in the shadows like some kind of creepy stalker. Eliza had nearly finished her cigarette and he was just skulking there like a lawn ornament. They had to be kept outside, a couple of tweaks to the faders on the mixing desk just put enough extra decibels into the beer garden to remind Eliza what she was missing, which fortunately persuaded her to stay outside for another cigarette.

Finally, it was a simple matter to stop the valve on her lighter. Now all that was left was for

Luke to reveal himself. I'd moved heaven and earth to make this moment happen. Starting with a man with a strange love of goldfish excrement, and setting up a whole chain of people being it the right place at the right time, all of it just so this could happen.

Luke stepped into the light, holding out his lighter and looking awkward.

CHAPTER TWENTY-TWO

Chance Encounters With Loaded Dice

There was a new arrival in the back 'o beyond, in the place where you go where you die. Some people called it the afterlife, some called it purgatory, some people who had too many cats and thought they "might be a bit psychic" called it the overly flowery "beyond the veil". The one thing that everyone seemed to agree on was that you couldn't call it heaven. The new arrival's name was Luke, and he was a particularly messy case. I watched him stumbling about, trying to figure out why his head was still attached to his neck, he exhibited all the classic signs of a newbie back here. It was my job to get him a bit of help to find the right track.

I left him to it, fairly sure he'd manage to avoid getting eaten or rolled in his first couple of hours, and paid a visit to the Wosh And Winse. I had friends there, or at least people who were willing to help me in exchange for useful information only I could provide. A little taste of the future got me access to their connections and influence. They had a dog who owed them a favour, and it was time to collect.

"OK, here's the deal." I passed them an envelope with very specific details of the locations of a number of people they were deeply interested in, "I want the JuJu Puppy to take on a case. He's a new arrival, and he has no clue what's going on. JuJu's going to take him under his wing, show him the ropes, and get him in shape. Then, he's going to help him get a job with the Authority, and become his official therapist and grief counsellor. And he's going to do all of this for free."

"Tell him he can try to get money out of the new guy if he wants - he can certainly invoice him for his time if that helps with his tax returns, but if the bills aren't paid then that's just the way it is - tell him he'll almost certainly be amply rewarded in free drinks, too. I can't imagine he'll have too much of a problem with that. If nothing else, he might just make a new friend, and a new drinking partner - everyone needs a good drinking companion, am I right?"

"Past that, I have an envelope that you need to give to him, with information about the case. That's for his eyes only." The Wongs nodded at me, accepted the envelope, and I left. I knew they wouldn't let me down - really they didn't have a choice.

I wanted to go and see the JuJu Puppy myself, but that dog always had a big mouth, and besides - he couldn't know how it was all going to pan out until the time was right. I wanted to buy him another drink, tell him I was sorry that I led him to where he ended up, and that I forgave him for his own betrayals. Unfortunately, it just wasn't an option, so our whole relationship was built on a manipulation.

The envelope contained a dossier on Loupe (Luke would think JuJu couldn't pronounce his name properly until it finally stuck, as these things often do - remember Joseph Pismel?), giving him enough information to allow him to easily manipulate me into making the decisions I had to make, to start on the trail of finding out how my son really died.

It also contained that key fact, that it was me who did it - well, kind of, it said that Luke had done it and then his mind had created the invisible monster to take the blame, a sort of supernatural one-armed man. Of course, JuJu didn't know it was me now, not the me then - but because he was a very good therapist, he was good enough to move me towards the truth at a pace that wouldn't drive me mad - a pace that would allow me to deal with what I had to do.

I wished I could have said more, and I wished I could have thanked him properly for what he sacrificed, and for a lot of nights in the bar that I enjoyed a lot more than I let on. Unfortunately, our paths couldn't cross in that way, and I had to finish what I started. Or start what I finished, depending on your point of view. Beginnings are pretty fluid things, in my experience, but where I was heading now was as good a beginning as any.

CHAPTER TWENTY-THREE

Looping The Loupe

And here we are, back at the hospital, all those years ago. I slip through the cracks and into the corridor. From a pair of swing doors thirty feet away, I hear screaming. I approach the doors and look through the round windows into the room beyond. My mother on the bed, bucking wildly in the grip of a seizure, her belly swollen with me, ready to come out. Well, not really me. Not yet. Nurses cluster around her, trying to calm her down, to get her under control.

Stood on the other side of the bed, looking down over her, is me. Well, me from a while ago. I wonder if I would have seen myself if I'd looked up at this window then? It's an easy enough thing to test - I look all around myself, a quick push backwards in time, and I'm stood next to myself as I look through the windows. Then I look all around, and vanish - looks like I can't see future me. Creepy. I could be stood right next to myself right now, and I wouldn't even know it. I turn back to the window.

My father is looking terrified as a doctor speaks to him off to one side, then takes him by the shoulder and leads him to the door. I step back, and lean against the wall as he's ushered out into the corridor to wait. The doors close behind him, flapping out and then back in before coming to a close - it's almost a comedy "don't let the door hit your arse on the way out" moment. I'm glad that didn't happen though, would have been inappropriate.

He turns and looks back at the door, taking half a step forward - then I guess the magnesium sulphate just went in, because a curdling wail rises from the room. He steps back, and bursts into tears. I walk over to him, put an arm around him, and lead him to some nearby seats. He sits, looking numb.

"Do you want a coffee? I think I saw a machine down the corridor."

"That would be... yes. Coffee."

"Oh. I haven't got any money."

He reaches into his pocket, pulls out a handful of change and shoves it into my hand without looking. His eyes are fixed on the doors in front of him, and he flinches at each scream from within. I pat him awkwardly on the shoulder, stand up, and head down the corridor to the grubby coffee machine. The coins rattle around in its innards, and in return it coughs up two phlegmy cups of brown. I return to where my dad sits. He takes one of the drinks, but doesn't drink it, just holds the cup in his hands. I sip mine, and wish I'd just held onto it instead.

"So, what's happening?"

"It's the baby. It's killing her. They think they're going to have to... intervene. But it's dangerous. She could die anyway, and the baby."

And then it hits me. All along I've been working with one assumption - that the baby in there right now is me. But I realise now that it isn't. Why can no-one else do the things I can do? Because they're human, and then when they die, they're post-human. That isn't what I am, I'm something... other than that. As for what, I don't think that's relevant, because now I realise that I'm in a position to do something. I turn to my dad, who isn't my father, but is my dad.

"I think I can help. I think I can save her, but I want your permission. Right now I'm a stranger to you, but you'll just have to believe that I have a lot invested in you - you could say my entire future depends on what you say now. I think I already know the answer. I don't think there's another answer you can give me. I need you to give me your son."

"Do it."

"You have to say the words."

"I..."

"Just say 'Take my son'"

He pauses for a moment, but only a breath. "Take him. Take my son."

I take the coffee from him, and place both cups on the floor. Then I take his hand and shake it firmly, sealing the deal, accepting the permission for what I'm about to do. Nobody really has any choice at this point anyway - I'm not going to kill his son because I want to. I didn't kill my son because I wanted to. I did it because that's what happens. This all might seem irrelevant, but I don't believe it is - I might not be human, I might be some other kind of entity - but I've lived my entire existence as a human and beyond into what comes after, so human or no - I still want to maintain my humanity.

Of course, my mother will know. When I'm born, she'll know, and she'll be the one who sees that shadow on me - the shadow of the child she carried, the wraith of the child I'm going to replace. Even though I'll do it to save her life, she won't forgive me, and she won't forgive herself for allowing it to happen - and nobody else will see the truth of it. I know I won't remember any of this, this final push, this final crime. But I know that the shadow that is born with me will remember, and will stick to me - that shadow is the blood that I can never wash off, the guilt of a crime I can forget, but can never erase. I'm the parasite, I'm the invader.

I have one more trick up my sleeve. I stand, and look down at my dad - then turn a corner of my mind, just so. And I'm gone. I turn to the door, and step through it. My mother is on the bed, the magnesium sulphate tearing through her blood vessels. The younger post-mortem me is stood on the other side of the bed, blissfully unaware of what I'm going to do, totally oblivious to my presence. I sit on the edge of the bed, as they come to take her to the OR, and as they prep her for surgery, as that baby prepares to finish her forever, I start my work.

I press against her side like a faith healer, rubbing and twisting, fingers gaining purchase in the soft flesh. First a digit, and then a hand, reaching in and searching for my new enemy. He detects the invasion, and though he doesn't recognise the threat he knows it for what it is - and he resists. My mother's heart skips a beat as we wage our war, as I try to get a grip on my wriggling foe. Finally, a finger hooks him, and I grab him. And I squeeze, pushing him out of the body that he's earned, creating a shell ready to be filled up... with me. I'm the cuckoo, pushing the eggs out of another bird's nest, ready to replace them with my own.

And I get ready to be born again, focusing myself into the little one that I've stolen, kicking and slapping him out of the way as he tries to regain the ground I've taken from him. He curls around me like smoke, and I can feel his rage boiling at the opportunity I've denied him. He tries to enter any way he can, but I'm too strong, I own this now, and I can wait to be born. My mind settles into the new flesh, not big enough to hold all of me - so I start to let pieces go, and they flutter away like fragments of burning photographs from a purifying bonfire. As for him, well I think he's coming with me - he's going to be the face that watches me out of that skylight, the monster in the airing cupboard, he's going to be the fear that follows me.

Nothing is brighter or sweeter than certainty, I can tell you that. I'm beyond any kind of worry right now - despite the things I've done, and the things I'll do again. The JuJu Puppy might not have been a fan of the predestined, but for me it's a blessed relief. Right now I feel like my face is in the sun for the first time, and I find it hard to believe there was ever anything else.

I am Loupe. I exist because I have to exist - I create myself anew time and over, and the big wheel turns, with me tied to the same spoke. I can't escape this any more than a confused moth can escape the pull of a light bulb, or an apple can escape the pull of gravity. I couldn't tell you if I'm governed by these natural forces, or if I am the natural force that shapes the events around me. Like that song - "when he's underwater does he get wet, or does the water get him instead?"

I am Luke. I exist because I have to exist - without me now, there can be no me that follows, and without the me that follows there can be no me now. The beginning and the ending are irrelevant, I always have been, always will be, and always must be. I am the chicken and the egg - the source and the destination, unlike other chickens, which come from an egg, which comes from something that is almost, but not quite, a chicken. There's a question for the philosophers, not for me - I'll ride the rollercoaster without worrying about the physics that keep me in my seat.

Perhaps I could make different decisions, but it's clear that I either don't, won't or can't - if I did then I wouldn't be here - so my path through life (if you can call it that) is inevitable. It may seem that it would be confusing, but with the absence of choice comes an equal absence of responsibility - and that's liberating by anyone's measure. Sure, until I got to this point it was tough but here, now... it's serene. I can float here until I'm good to go.

The loop is closing, and I feel myself disappearing into this new form. I'll be born again, back then and start the story once again. Who knows where I came from? More importantly, who cares? I just am, and I'll keep going round my little patch of space and time, making the same mistakes, because when I get to here each time it'll be worthwhile. Because this moment, this feeling right here and now? It's a magical moment of nirvana, of acceptance. It's the moment of weightlessness at the apex of a jump. It's the breath you hold as your finger tightens on the trigger. My little loop has tied a noose around reality at that point, and the pressure it creates will resist their tireless quest for order - and good, because order isn't the natural state of universe.

I can see the lines that Gaunt and Nathaniel spoke about, the strings that tie each human soul together, all pulled tight, gathered into one point - this point, here and now. I don't know if all the people in the world can feel it - maybe it creates a point of synchronicity for each of them, maybe right now everyone on earth is thinking the same thought, feeling the same feeling, just for this instant. All of these realities dragged together into a point of almost unbearable pressure. When I take that step, when I finish this, those lines, those connections - at least for now - will spring out from this point in all directions. They'll cross and tangle and dance and every person on each of those lines will be able to choose their own path, and make their own destinies. It's a sundering of the Authority's work so complete they won't be able to undo it in a thousand lifetimes.

Maybe this is what it's like for everyone, but I suspect not. I'm sure this isn't what the JuJu Puppy had in mind when he said he wanted me to move on - I think other people get something else, maybe they just cease to be, maybe there's more reality yet to be seen. But for me, this is what I get, I get certainty, one glorious moment of acceptance - if that isn't the definition of moving on, of dealing with your unfinished business, then I don't know what is.

As for my crimes, the lives I've taken, the lives I've ruined... you can seek forgiveness from all the people you've wronged in the world. Maybe Eliza won't forgive me, but we'll get another chance to make the same mistakes. Maybe my parents won't forgive me, but he made his choice, and if it hadn't been for me, she would have died. Maybe no-one will forgive me, but there's a simpler solution. If you forgive yourself, then no-one else's opinion matters, and so before I go on, I absolve myself of all the crimes I've committed. It's really that easy.

I'm sorry, I'm already starting to forget this story, I'm trying to hold on to at least some it, some knowledge that will guide me through the life ahead. I know I can't - it's futile, because I know I don't remember anything. So I let it go. Not to worry, I'll get to know it all again. I am infinite. I am Loupe.

EPILOGUE

What Happens When The Dead Die?

As you might expect, it's never really over.
Reality goes deeper and further than you can
ever see, a fractal expansion from the origin.
Just like in life, all the best questions don't even
have answers, just more questions. Like a
drawing popped into full existence, you keep
moving forwards, expanding in all directions,
plotting yourself along a new axis you didn't
know existed before.

Of course, if you put a piece of paper on a table,
the drawing on that paper can only see itself
within the boundaries of it's own two
dimensional space, but the paper and everything
on it is perfectly visible in the wider context of
the room in which it sits. When the living die,
they get kicked off the page, and find themselves
in the room. When the dead die, the same thing
happens - suddenly you can see the house, and
look through the windows into the room.
There's always something more to see - I
suppose it's a bit like Disneyland in that respect.

So perhaps this is the way of it, transcendence event stacked on transcendence event. Maybe somewhere out there in the universe there are mystical beings beyond our comprehension looking at each other and saying, yeah look at that thing spiral away, do you ever wonder what it's made of? Well, George, basically it's just a giant stack of gods all the way down. It's possible that one day we'll all get a turn at running the show. Something tells me it will take forever to get there, though, so I'll just keep taking it one day at a time.

The further out you go, the easier it is too see the patterns of causality unfold through the universe, and you can just reach out and tweak it, just like that. Of course, it's no fun to go straight to the changes you want. What is fun is building machines, complex little Rube Goldberg sequences of events that end in the desired effect. It's strange to think of myself as the author of my own destiny, and that I've been a part of shaping the events that got me here after the fact. Like so much in the universe, it's better not to think about it too hard. Just accept that the great jigsaw doesn't always fit together in the way you thought it did, and leave it at that.

Circles within spirals, wheels within wheels, other hippy-dippy lyrics that a deceased dog can steal. I don't doubt for a second that my own decisions here have been influenced in the same way, by someone else pulling the strings and pushing the buttons. The chances are that whoever is doing that is just as much the puppet of some other bored entity. Gods all the way down, gods all the way up - maybe there's someone or something right up at the top controlling the whole thing like some kind of ludicrously complex video game. Even if that's the case, the question of who wrote the game code in the first place still stands.

Loupe could have gone either way, and he just needed a little push, one domino dropping in his path at just the right moment. All I had to do was get that domino in the right place at the right time - and like all the best games, you score more points if you take the most convoluted path to victory possible. Yeah fine, it's a score I'm making up for a game I'm inventing for myself but that's the way it is, we have to make our own entertainment up here.

Zeus and his mates had no problem with sitting around the celestial chessboard toying with the destinies of the mortals - and since the little people get their own turn at the game, it doesn't seem particularly unfair. Job done, high score. Now... who fancies a drink? I'm gasping. I don't know what I'll do if I ever end up in some dimensional loophole without a decent bar.

Juju out.